PRAISE FOR

Here are some of the over 100,000 five star reviews left for the Dead Cold Mystery series.

"Rex Stout and Michael Connelly have spawned a protege."

AMAZON REVIEW

"So begins one damned fine read."

AMAZON REVIEW

"Mystery that's more brain than brawn."

AMAZON REVIEW

"I read so many of this genre...and ever so often I strike gold!"

AMAZON REVIEW

"This book is filled with action, intrigue, espionage, and everything else lovers of a good thriller want."

AMAZON REVIEW

THE SINS OF THE FATHER

A DEAD COLD MYSTERY

BLAKE BANNER

RIGHTHOUSE

ISBN-13: 978-1-63696-005-0

ISBN-10: 1-63696-005-7

Cover design by: Damonza

Printed in the United States of America

www.righthouse.com

www.instagram.com/righthousebooks

www.facebook.com/righthousebooks

twitter.com/righthousebooks

DEAD COLD MYSTERY SERIES

ONE

"This one."

She had her boots crossed on the corner of the desk, at the end of her mile-long legs, and she was leaning back in a pool of lazy September sunshine. She threw the file she had been reading on the desk in front of me.

I sighed and dropped the one I'd been reading—a disemboweled mob lawyer—into the "maybe later" pile and picked up her folder from the desk. She closed her eyes and made a temple of her fingers, as though she were Sherlock Holmes. I was struck, not for the first or last time, by how exquisite her face was. She opened one eye and raised that eyebrow at me. "Are you going to read it?"

I sat back and put my ankles on the desk next to hers.

"Simon Martin, thirty-two, beaten and stabbed during a home invasion on the fifth of September, 1999, Bogart Avenue. That's not far from here. Victim had just got home from work. He had bruising to the ribs and a jaw break consistent with having been punched, and he had been stabbed in the chest with a very large knife. Weapon was *not* found. Wife, Sylvie, was apparently upstairs at the time of the assault, but suffered shock-induced amnesia, so was unable to give a statement . . ." I gave Dehan a skeptical glance, but her eyes were still closed. I continued. "There were no signs of forced entry. The back door was unlocked, and there were footprints in the garden from common white tennis shoes, size ten or eleven. You awake?"

"I'm listening."

"You can't look and listen at the same time? I thought women were supposed to be good at multitasking."

She opened her eyes and revealed a total lack of humor. "Really, Stone? Sexist stereotyping, now, are we? That is so typical of a man. The more sensory input you can shut down, the more you are able to focus."

I ignored her and looked back at the file, glancing through the pages. "Okay. Yeah, let's do it."

"You're not going to read the rest of the file?"

"Tell me about it as we go."

As we stepped out into the early afternoon, she said, "You know, Stone, you are not an unattractive man."

I frowned at her. We crossed the road toward my burgundy 1964 Jaguar Mark II and I thought absently that it was not an unattractive car.

Dehan continued, which was a little unsettling. "You are not unlike the man, Bogart."

"Knock it awf, shweetheart."

I unlocked the car and climbed in.

As she got in the passenger seat, she said, "I'm serious. You're taller—what are you, six two?"

"Six one."

"Perhaps Harrison Ford or Hugh Jackman would be a better comparison."

I reversed out of the lot and pulled onto Storey Avenue, headed east. I settled back in my seat and scowled. "Dehan," I said with a degree of severity. "I know what you are doing. The answer is no, I do not want a woman in my life. What is it with you and trying to get me paired up?"

"I don't know, Stone. You're a good-looking guy, you're comparatively young . . ."

"Thanks."

"You're one of the good guys, and believe me, that is *rare*. It just seems like a waste that you are single. It's a shame."

"We have had this conversation before. And besides, I could say the same about you. Only you are not a good-looking guy. You are . . ." I waved my hand around, realizing the conversation was getting into dangerous waters. "Anyway, the fact is we would probably both make terrible husbands and wives."

She shrugged. "You would be a terrible wife. I would probably be a pretty good husband."

"You are a very disturbing woman."

She sighed. "That is what my shrink keeps telling me."

I took Rosedale North as far as East Tremont, then turned left onto Bronxdale and right onto Pierce. Bogart was the second on the left. I parked outside the Martins' house and looked at Dehan. She seemed abstracted. I smiled. "I'm glad it was Bogart Avenue and not Karloff."

She gave a sad smile and climbed out.

There was a fish sticker in the window that told me that Jesus loved me. Another one told me that even though I did not believe in God, God believed in me. I was pretty sure they were both wrong. Dehan came up beside me and commented, "If they keep putting up enlightening stickers, they are going to block out the light."

"Droll."

I rang the bell and knocked on the door. Almost like a weird coincidence, the neighbor's door opened, and a woman with a very large, nosy air about her looked at me like she wanted to accuse me of something but didn't know what yet.

"They ain't in."

I smiled the smile of an innocent man and said, "Where are they?"

"Church. They are always at church."

I nodded. "Of course. Can you tell me where the church is?"

She smiled unexpectedly and looked a hundred years younger.

"Out back." She pointed, in case I didn't know where out back was. "Fowler Avenue. Right at the back, here . . . You can walk it."

I thanked her again, and we descended the steps we had recently just climbed up. It was a three-hundred-yard stroll through an odd neighborhood that blended leafy trees in the first russet shades of fall with very homey redbrick houses and soulless concrete yards fenced with steel tubing and wire mesh. The overall vibe was a very unhappy one.

The church was small and, judging by the design, early-twentieth-century Methodist. It was a sturdy redbrick building with towering Gothic arches and a rotund tower at the very back. It stood in its own grounds, surrounded by towering maple trees and gloomy-looking chestnut trees. There was a cute redbrick rectory on the left. The door, which stood open, was now dull, but once must have been a vibrant red, with a set of heavy, black iron hinges. A flagged path led to a small graveyard on the right, and beyond that there was a large garden. There, some kind of church fête seemed to be in progress. There was bunting strung from the trees, and there were stalls selling secondhand clothes, books, vinyl records, record players, and old rusty tools, as well as homemade lemonade, chocolate brownies, cookies, and cakes. There was a big crowd swirling around the church grounds.

We strolled in among the throng of people and headed for the cake stall. It was attended by a pretty, blond woman who must have been in her late thirties, and a pretty girl who had to be her daughter stood beside her. She was probably in her late teens or early twenties. They both gave us bright smiles that looked as though they belonged in the South, where life was good and morality was uncomplicated.

"Hi there!" It was the woman. She said it like we were old friends, and for a moment I wondered if I knew her. "Welcome! Can we offer you some amazing lemonade?"

Dehan answered before I could draw breath. "You sure can, and we'll have a couple of those brownies too."

The daughter poured while the mother shoveled. I took my

brownie from her and said, "Maybe you can help us. We are actually looking for somebody."

"Oh." She seemed genuinely pleased at the possibility of being able to help. "Well, we know most everyone around here, don't we, honey?"

Her daughter nodded and also looked equally as eager to help. Dehan said, "Sylvie Martin?"

They were thrilled, and I swear the mother gave a little jump. "Oh, well, that's me! I am Sylvie Martin!" She took hold of her daughter and added, "And this is Mary, my daughter! How can we help you?"

Dehan's mouth was full of chocolate brownie, so all she could say was, "Umph . . ."

I took over, with what is generally termed as "an easy smile." "We are police officers." I put down my lemonade, fished out my badge, and showed it to her. "I am Detective John Stone, and this is my partner, Detective Carmen Dehan."

A hint of a frown, the smile strained almost imperceptibly by concern as soon as the words "police officer" hit her ears.

"Oh, is there a problem . . . ?"

"No." I shook my head and bit into the brownie. It was good, and I allowed my face to say so. Speaking with my mouth full, I said, "It is the policy of the Forty-Third Precinct to review cold cases from time to time, Mrs. Martin, and we are currently conducting a review of . . ."

I trailed off. She had gone very pale. Her daughter was watching her and had placed her hand on her shoulder. Sylvie said, "I thought that was a permanently closed case."

Dehan swallowed the last of her brownie and said, "Simon's murderer is still at large, Sylvie. The case can't be closed."

"I would . . . We would all, really, rather put the whole thing behind us. The Lord dispenses His own justice."

"I'm sorry, Mrs. Martin." I meant it; she looked genuinely distressed. "But we have to do our job. Is there somewhere we can talk privately?"

She gave a deep sigh and searched the crowd for a moment. Then she raised a hand and called, "Oh, Paul . . . Reverend Truelove . . . !"

I turned and watched a large, leonine man, with silver hair swept back from his head in a perfect swoop, move through the crowd toward us. He looked for a moment like a Spanish galleon parting the seas in some forgotten, surrealist book of the Old Testament. He graced us both with the bounty of his kind smile, lingering a little longer and with more bounty upon the beautiful Dehan than on me. Finally, he turned to Sylvie Martin.

"Sylvie, who are your friends?" Then, turning to us again, he said, "Welcome to St. George's." He had a voice like a particularly excellent church organ.

I showed him my badge. "Detectives Stone and Dehan, NYPD. Superb brownies and lemonade, by the way. We were wondering if we could borrow Sylvie for five minutes. It is purely a formality. We are reviewing a cold case . . ."

He frowned. "A cold case? You can't mean poor Simon, surely?"

Dehan, with her usual directness, asked, "Why not?"

"Well." He smiled. "That must be sixteen or seventeen years ago."

"Eighteen, but it is still unsolved." She grinned. "So we keep working at solving it until we bring him justice."

"I see." He frowned as though he did not agree. "Well, that is very commendable. By all means, would you like to use the vestry?" He gestured with his hand, ushering us in that direction. Turning to Sylvie's daughter, he said, "Mary, you'll tend the stall for a moment, won't you?"

She smiled. "Of course, Reverend."

Sylvie Martin led us down the side of the church, under the shadow of the trees, toward the side door into the nave, and all the way I could feel Reverend Paul Truelove's eyes burning on my back.

TWO

THE INSIDE OF THE CHURCH WAS DARK BY CONTRAST with the bright sunshine outside. The Gothic arch of the doorway, on the far right, was startling, luminous in red and green. And on the left, there was the tenuous flicker of candles by the altar. Sylvie crossed herself and led us from the transept to another perfectly arched, wooden door that gave on to the vestry at the back of the altar.

We followed her into a comfortable room that had the feel of an old-world library or study. There was an oak desk, a two-seater sofa, and a couple of black leather chairs. Two tall, frosted windows looked out onto the colorful fête outside. Sylvie sat on the sofa with her knees together and bent them slightly to one side. Dehan and I took the chairs. I smiled in a way I hoped was reassuring.

"Mrs. Martin . . ."

"Sylvie, please."

"Sylvie. We understand that this must be difficult, and the last thing we want to do is stir up any painful memories. But you understand, a serious crime has been committed, and we are obliged to investigate."

She nodded. "Yes, of course I understand. I will try to help in any way that I can, I mean if I can . . ."

"What can you tell us about the events of that evening?"

She placed her hands, one on top of the other, on her lap and looked at them sadly, as though they had disappointed her somehow.

"My memory . . ." she said. "My memory of that evening is practically nonexistent, if I am being honest. I just seemed to black out at the time, and it has never come back."

Dehan said, "Don't worry. Don't force yourself. How about the hour or two before?"

She smiled briefly at Dehan and said, "Um . . . I had fed and changed Mary. She was just one at the time. Ahmed had come over from the church . . ."

"Ahmed?"

"He was a refugee, a young Arab boy, from Iraq. He was just sixteen, and Paul—that's Reverend Truelove—had offered him some work at the church to give him a hand in making ends meet. Odd jobs, gardening and whatnot. We all hoped he would find the true faith, but we never pressured him."

I frowned. "And he had come over to your house?"

"Simon had offered him work too, in the garden, a few after-noons a week."

Dehan sat forward. "So you had fed and changed Mary, and then Ahmed had come over and he was working in the garden."

"Yes . . ."

"What happened next?"

Her face seemed to go tight. Her fingers closed on the hem of her dress. "I suppose it must have gotten dark. I am not sure. I know Simon came home from work. I remember he was calling to say he was home, but none of the lights were on in the house. I hate to waste electricity, you see, but I remember that the kitchen door out into the garden was open. I remember that without a doubt. I know I was sitting on the bottom of the stairs and the house was completely dark and still. I felt a bit cold. And Simon was lying there, in his coat. His briefcase was next to him and he was staring straight up at the ceiling."

She frowned, as though she was trying to remember something, and I was surprised to realize she was crying. She held her breath for a moment, and suddenly she was like a woman with a bad cold. I reached over and handed her my handkerchief, and Dehan moved and sat next to her, putting her arm around her shoulders.

"Where was Ahmed?"

"Gone. Gone before the dusk."

"I know it is hard, but please try to remember. Did anybody else call?"

"I don't know. The kitchen door was open, into the garden."

I smiled at her. "Do you come from Texas?"

She gave a small, damp laugh. "Is it that obvious?"

"Y'all still got the twang."

She laughed and wagged a finger at me. "Y'all ain't never singular, Detective Stone. Y'all best remember that!" She fiddled with the handkerchief for a moment, then said, "Simon worked at Federal United. They transferred him here. We didn't really want to leave Austin, we liked it there, but it was a chance for a promotion and more money . . ." She shrugged. "So we took it. We could have gone to Brooklyn. The bank offered us a place there. But Simon said we could do more good through the church here, where there was more need."

For a moment, I was reminded of the stickers in her window, but I didn't mention them. Instead, I asked her, "Who alerted the police?"

She stared at me. It was an odd expression, almost apologetic. "I had the phone in my hand . . . It must have been me."

Dehan stroked her back a couple of times. "Did you speak to him?" Sylvie turned to look at her. Dehan went on, "He called to you to let you know he was home. Did you answer? Did you say anything?"

Her bottom lip began to quiver. She made a strange, guttural sound like, "Oh, God . . . !" and collapsed against her, sobbing. Dehan enfolded her in her arms and looked at me, shaking her head.

I sat for a moment, watching her and thinking. When she had settled a bit, I said, "We won't trouble you any more today, Sylvie, but we may want to talk to you again as the investigation progresses. I do understand it's hard, but I would like you to give some thought to Detective Dehan's questions and see if anything begins to surface in your memory. Can you do that for me?"

She nodded, blinking, and blew her nose. "I'm sorry."

I stood. "No need to be at all."

"I suppose I had better get back to my daughter."

I smiled. "Y'all take care, y'hear?"

She laughed sadly and we followed her out into the nave. As we approached the transept, a shadow moved across the door at the far end, and a foot seemed to scuff the stone floor, setting up an echo in the vaulted ceiling. Sylvie stopped and peered, and blew her nose.

"Humberto?" The figure shuffled closer. Dehan glanced at me. Sylvie said again, "Humberto, is that you?"

He was tall, almost seven feet, and massive, though he stooped and had a shambling gait. Slowly, he came into the diffuse light of the candles. His features were hard to make out with the glare of sunlight behind him, but his face was broad, his jaw was big, and his brow was low on his face. He was grinning as he came closer. Both his grin and his steps were hesitant. When he spoke, his voice was nasally.

"*Donna Maria, benedicta santisima, purisima mater nostra . . .*" He laughed nervously, making a sound like a braying ass, knocked his knees, and gripped his crotch with both hands. "*Perdonattame, perdonattame . . .*"

She smiled at him. "It's okay, Humberto, you can sit and pray, *orare, orare,* you can sit."

He brayed again, biting his lower lip. "*Santisima madre, benedita, plena di grattia . . .*"

He backed away and after a couple of steps turned and dashed off into the shadows among the rear pews. Sylvie opened the side door at the end of the transept and we stepped out into the sunshine. Dehan asked it. She had to, and I knew it was killing her to know.

"Who is that?"

"Humberto?" Sylvie shrugged. "He's attached to Paul . . ." She sighed. "Sorry, Reverend Truelove. Nobody really knows his story. He just seems always to have been here. I suspect the reverend adopted him at some point, but he's so humble, he never talks about it." She shrugged. "Either way, he has found a home, literally, in the church."

I frowned. "What is that language he speaks? It's not Latin or Italian."

She laughed. "It is some kind of peculiar invention of his own. It's a generic Latin. People have identified Portuguese, Italian, Spanish, modern Latin, and classical Latin, plus a good few inventions of his own. He seems to make it up as he goes along."

"How old is he?"

She shrugged and shook her head. "Nobody knows."

I saw the reverend walking toward us. Sylvie held up the handkerchief. "I will wash it and return it to you when you are around next. Thank you for being so understanding. I'd better go."

She had taken less than a dozen paces when she and the reverend crossed. We watched as he stopped and took hold of her shoulders. They looked into each other's faces but they did not speak. After a moment, he patted her on the arm and she moved off in the direction of her stall, and Reverend Truelove—Paul—approached us with the walk of a man who owns a God who owns the world.

Without preamble, he said, "It was almost two decades ago, but to her it's as raw and livid as though it had happened today, five minutes ago."

"The mind is its own place, reverend, and can make a heaven of hell, a hell of heaven."

He looked at me curiously. "Indeed. Was she able to help any? It was a long time ago. Memories fade . . ."

Dehan scratched her head. "Well, Reverend, from what you just said, it was a long time ago for you, but not for her. So her memory hasn't faded." She affected the accent of the Deep South. "The mind bein' its own place, an' all." She pointed at the large group of people milling among the stalls. There were perhaps eighty or a hundred of them. "See those people, Reverend? How many of them do you reckon were here eighteen years ago?"

He looked startled. "I am not sure. Most of them, I should think."

"And how many of them, would you say, knew for sure that Sylvie's kitchen door was open that evening?"

His jaw dropped and he stared at her in astonishment.

She plowed on. "Because, Reverend, in that—much smaller—group, you will probably find a man who wanted to kill Simon Martin." She smiled. "Kind of changes things, doesn't it? Bit less vague and a bit more immediate."

He did the goldfish thing of staring with big eyes and sound-lessly opening and closing his mouth.

I smiled at him and asked, "Were you here that evening, Reverend?"

"Why . . . yes, um, I'm not sure . . . No." He shook his head. "I truly don't recall."

I shrugged. "It's a long time ago. I just thought, given the events of the night . . ."

"Oh, quite so. It just escapes my mind at the moment. I can tell you that I didn't find out what had happened until the next morning. But for the life of me . . ." He hesitated. "It was a terrible shock, of course. I felt somehow guilty that I hadn't been here for her at the time . . ."

I nodded, then gave a small, sideways twitch of my head. "You can hardly be held responsible for that. What kind of man was Simon? Do you know of any enemies he might have had?"

He puffed out his cheeks. "It is hard to imagine such a thing. He was a committed Christian, and a genuinely good man." He gave a knowing smile, inviting us to join him in a cozy joke. "Because, as we know, there are many committed Christians, who are not necessarily genuinely good people."

Dehan snorted. "You got that right."

He raised an eyebrow at her that said he found her vaguely distasteful, then addressed me. "He was a serious man, did not invite easy friendship, but he was very upright and did a great deal for charity, and for the church."

I scratched my chin. "I have to ask this, Reverend, and I hope you understand that there is nothing to be gained by concealing the truth through a misguided sense of loyalty." He looked affronted, but I ignored him and carried on. "How were things at home between Simon and Sylvie?"

He looked grave. "To be honest, a little joyless. Simon was a very devout man who saw little point in having fun. Joy, in his view, was to be achieved exclusively through an undivided devotion to God." He sighed and spread his hands. "Sylvie is a joyful, happy soul, and I fear she was withering a little in their marriage." He smiled beatifically. "Of course, Mary brought her much joy and laughter while Simon was at work, but, well, their life together was serious and contemplative, rather than gay and exuberant." He smiled thinly at Dehan. "I use the word gay in its true meaning, of course."

I nodded. "Would you have described Sylvie as frustrated back then?"

He looked uncomfortable. "I don't know that I would have chosen *that* particular word, but let's say I would not have described her as *fulfilled*. However, certainly not frustrated to the point of *homicide*, if that is what you are getting at."

I shook my head. "I am not driving at anything, Reverend,

just trying to understand the situation. We have no suspects yet at this time, unfortunately."

Dehan frowned. "One last question and then we'll leave you in peace . . . for a bit. Does Sylvie have a job . . . ?" She shrugged, shook her head, and spread her hands all at the same time. "What is her source of income?"

"Simon had made a very generous cushion, if you will, for her by means of a couple of insurance policies. That was him all over. So she works full time, on a voluntary basis, at the church. To be working in God's service helps her to heal from what happened so many years ago."

I held out my hand. "Thank you, Reverend. We'll try not to disturb you unnecessarily, but we will need to talk to you again at some point during this investigation."

He took my hand in both of his and held it tight. "Well, naturally, any help we can offer you, we will be only too glad to assist. But I have to say, Detective, it has taken Sylvie a long time to get back on her feet. We have all been there for her, to help and support her through very dark times. It would be a shame if, in seeking Simon's killer, you reopened wounds that are only just beginning to heal."

"I hear you, Reverend. We will be as sensitive as we can."

We shook hands and made our way back to the car.

THREE

INSTEAD OF GOING BACK TO THE PRECINCT, I TURNED right on Van Nest and then left onto Paulding and pulled up in front of Doyle's Pub. We grabbed a couple of beers and went to sit at a small table by the window. Dehan started talking while I took a pull and wiped the froth from my mouth.

"Okay, brief review of the facts: Sylvie is home alone with her newborn, Mary. The kid, Ahmed, is out in the garden doing the gardening. Neighbors—and you would know this if you had read the file—reported that they saw Simon arrive home in his car shortly after seven."

She paused to drink, smacked her lips, and sighed. I interrupted her.

"He lets himself in and finds that the lights are off. She made a point of that and she is not there to greet him. He was the kind of man, I suspect, who would have expected his wife to be there to greet him, with his dinner ready. But she said she heard him calling out for her."

"So why were the lights off and . . ."

I pulled a face. "I don't like 'why.' It is too open. What was it that stopped her from putting on the lights, as she would normally have done? Focuses the question a lot more keenly.

What was it that stopped her from being at the door when he arrived? I wonder if there was a meal being cooked . . ."

"You done, Sensei?"

I nodded.

"So, something unusual has happened *before* Simon gets home that has prevented his good wife from preparing for his homecoming." She raised a finger. "Now, things happen pretty quick at this point. Simon is struck forcefully in the ribs and on the jaw. The medic's report says he was bruised, premortem, on his left floating ribs and on the left side of his mandible. Which may have caused him to collapse on the floor. He was found still wearing his coat, stabbed in the chest, and, as Sylvie said, with his briefcase still by his side. All of which suggests he was barely through the door when he was attacked and murdered."

"You said stabbed in the chest, not stabbed in the heart."

"Yes. He was stabbed right through the sternum, at the height of the third intercostals."

"Through the sternum? You're sure?"

She raised an eyebrow. "What do you think? You think I'm sure?"

"I think you're sure."

"The blow must have been delivered with considerable force, which adds weight to the theory that he was lying on his back at the time he was stabbed. So his assailant was able to put all their weight behind the knife."

"Okay, so the picture suggests that the killer was the unknown element that prevented Sylvie from putting on the lights and dutifully greeting Simon at the door. And as soon as he came in, the killer struck. The position of the body was, if I am not mistaken, at the foot of the stairs . . ."

"Correct, which would suggest that the killer was either on the stairs or up the stairs when Simon came in the door."

"And from what Sylvie has told us, she was found sitting on the stairs, with the telephone in her hands. The actions around the trauma all center around the stairs."

Dehan nodded. "The 911 call was made from the phone she was holding."

I stared at the dry rings on the mahogany tabletop, seeing my imagined version of the Martins' entrance hall. "So the idea is that Sylvie is being held upstairs by the killer. Simon comes home, calls her, and the killer rushes down, punches him twice with his right fist, first in the ribs and then on the jaw, and, when he falls to the ground, he sits on him and stabs him through the sternum." I frowned at Dehan. "How many stab wounds?"

She smiled. "I was wondering when you'd ask that. Two."

"Hmmm . . . So our killer is in a bit of a frenzy and is certainly not a seasoned assassin. He has delivered two blows where one would have been ample, and he has stabbed him in the most difficult place on the chest. While, presumably, Sylvie is standing on the stairs watching him. It is very odd."

She turned her glass around a few times on the table, like she was trying to screw it down, or wind it up. After a moment, she said, "You're not wrong. I keep asking myself, 'Where was the phone?'"

She looked up at me and I nodded. It was what I had been asking myself too.

She went on, "What did she do? Stand there and watch her husband get murdered, then go to fetch the phone and return to sit on the stairs to call 911?"

I pulled a face, like I knew I wasn't convincing her and I wasn't really convincing myself either. "Maybe it was upstairs."

She echoed my expression with a shrug. "Maybe. Same thing applies. Anyway, motive and opportunity: prima facie . . ."

I smiled. "I like that. That's good. Prima facie. It's nice."

"You like that? It's good, huh? Thank you. So, prima facie, the only motive we can be sure of is Sylvie's."

"The life insurance."

"It has got to be pretty generous because it is paying either for the rent on a substantial house, or the mortgage. Plus, it's giving her enough to live on without having to work. If, on top of that, he was a miserable bastard to be married to . . ."

"That is a big assumption, Dehan."

She offered me a smile that was richer in scorn than in mirth. "Come on! He saw 'little point in fun,' and 'joy was to be achieved exclusively through devotion to God.' I call that being a miserable bastard. And remember . . ." She wagged a finger at me. "For a woman like Sylvie, divorce is not an option. The vow is 'till death do us part,' and God holds them to that. The penalty is not just hell, but being ostracized by their community. Hell is just an imagined future. Being reviled and ostracized is a hard reality to live with, especially for someone like Sylvie."

"So she was stuck with him for life."

"For the next sixty years."

"Unless . . ."

"Unless he died before that. Drink up. The next ones are on me."

"I have to drive."

"We are a ten-minute walk from your house. We'll be having spaghetti tonight."

"We are? Okay, sounds great to me."

I watched the streetlights come on through the darkening glass in the windows, and the attitude of people's walk shift from a businesslike stride to a homeward hurry as evening enclosed around them, past parking cars with amber headlamps. I thought of Sylvie, curled helpless against Dehan's shoulder, weeping, hiding from the truth in the shadows of amnesia.

Dehan sat and placed a glass in front of me. "I know what you're going to say," she said. "Sylvie hasn't the strength, either physical or of character, to knock her husband to the ground and stab him twice through the sternum. And I would have to agree. But that doesn't take away the fact that, so far, she is the only person with an apparent motive."

I took another pull on the beer. "So are we talking about an accomplice? That would imply a second motive."

"Do you ever wish you smoked, Stone?"

"Sometimes."

"Right now I could definitely use a cigarette."

"I read that nicotine helps ward off Alzheimer's."

"He didn't actually have the disease. It wasn't his."

"No, he just discovered it."

"So, who else stood to gain by Simon's death, Stone? The kid, Mary, was only about one year old. Reverend Paul Truelove?"

"Love? Sex? If that's the case, why haven't they gotten together since?"

She shrugged and sipped, then shrugged again as she put down the glass. "Maybe her Christian guilt kicked in and she repented after the deed was done. But we might equally ask, how come she hasn't gone back to Texas? Remember, Reverend Truelove was keen for us not to pursue the investigation because, and I quote, she was 'healing, working for God.'"

"Good points all three. Plus, he has no alibi for the night in question. Still, this is mere surmise at this stage; we need hard evidence to make it stick."

"I will contact her insurance company tomorrow and see how big the payout was."

I turned it over a few times in my mind with my glass halfway to my mouth. I spoke absently, half to myself, "I want to talk to the first emergency responders too. I'm interested in the wound. It might have more to tell us . . ."

Walking toward my house about half an hour later, through quiet, lamplit streets, Dehan said, "I guess if either one of us was in a relationship, we couldn't do this anymore, huh?"

I looked at her with big eyes. "Do what?"

"I mean, me stay over in your guest room, have dinner and breakfast . . . A husband or a wife would make that kind of hard."

I gave a small laugh. "Are you brooding, Dehan? What's eating you today?"

"Nothing! I'm just wondering. Jeez . . . I'm Jewish already! We overthink everything. It's part of our purpose in the world.

Other people don't think enough, so we overthink to compensate . . ."

"You're babbling again."

"We do that too."

"Are you trying to tell me you met someone?"

"No!"

The expression of horror on her face made me laugh. "It's okay if you did, it's cool. Everything is cool."

She spoke to her boots. "I just keep wondering why you haven't."

THINGS DIDN'T GO EXACTLY as planned the next morning. As I sat down behind my desk at eight a.m., my phone rang.

"Stone."

I saw Dehan roll her eyes and frown-shrugged "what?" at her. She made a face like a gorilla answering the phone and mouthed, "Stone!"

I turned away because Reverend Paul Truelove was talking to me.

"Ah, Detective Stone, I am glad to catch you early. I was wondering if I might come in and have a chat with you."

"Of course. What's it about?"

"So, would half an hour suit you?"

"Just fine. See you then."

Dehan was typing. She said, "Who?" to the screen.

"Reverend Truelove. Wants to have a chat in half an hour. He's on his way already, apparently."

She smiled and raised an eyebrow. "Hmmm . . ."

"What are you doing?"

She picked up her phone and dialed. "Insurance." She stood up and walked away on very long, slim legs. I called Frank.

"Hey, Frank, Stone here. How is it hanging?"

"Loose. What can I do for you?"

"Fifth September, 1999. Simon Martin. Stabbed through the sternum, twice, does that ring any bells?"

His laugh was mirthless. "You know how many stabbings we've had in the last eighteen years, Stone?"

"No. Can you look it up? Maybe even scare up the pathologist who did the report by this afternoon?"

"Yes, maybe, no. Yes, I can look it up. Maybe I can scare up the pathologist if he, she, or it is still in a condition to be scared. No, I can't do it by this afternoon. I'll call you when I have looked into it."

"I appreciate it."

"No, you don't. You take me for granted."

"You're right. I do, I'm sorry."

He hung up.

Dehan was strolling back across the room, listening carefully to her cell. She spoke briefly, giving her email address. Then she sat, hung up, and reached behind her head to tie her hair in a knot at the back of her neck.

"He had two insurance policies. The first covered the mortgage on the house in the event of his death. Which means that she basically got the house without having to pay for it. The second gave her an income for life of five thousand dollars a month; so sixty grand a year."

"Holy cow. That's like having a million bucks in the bank and living off the interest."

She leaned back in her chair and picked up a pencil, which she put in her mouth as though it were a cheroot. "I have a perfect life. The only problem is this pain in the ass of a husband who keeps pissing on my parade. Now, to make matters worse, he has taken out two insurance policies that make him totally redundant."

I thought for a moment and wagged a finger at her. "We need to take a closer look at the nature of those bruises. Frank is looking up the case. He's going to get back to me." I checked my watch. "Let's grab some coffee before the reverend gets here."

FOUR

REVEREND TRUELOVE ARRIVED ON TIME AND WAS shown into interview room three. That seemed to surprise him. As we sat down opposite, he smiled nervously at both of us.

"It feels as though I am being interrogated." Then he laughed like he was inviting us to tell him he was being ridiculous.

I gave him a second and said, in a neutral voice, "It's just a little more private than the main lounge."

"Of course."

Dehan leaned her elbows on the table. "So what did you want to tell us, Reverend?"

He laid his hands flat on the table and spread his fingers, looking at them like he was counting how many he had. He spoke carefully. "It is about where I was that evening, the evening of the murder, I mean."

"You said you didn't remember."

He raised his eyes and spoke to me, even though it was Dehan who'd made the comment. "The question took me somewhat by surprise. But reflecting afterwards, I recalled, of course, I had been to dinner with friends. Which was why I could not be there for poor Sylvie that night."

Dehan reclaimed his attention. "Do you mind telling us who those friends were?"

"No, of course not. I was dining with the Cavendishes, at their home in Eastchester Bay. I did not get home till midnight, and went straight to bed."

I said, "You understand we will have to check with them. It's not that we don't believe you." I smiled. "It's just that we are obliged to check."

"Naturally, Detective. I don't expect to be treated differently than anybody else."

Dehan gave a small, humorless laugh. "You won't be. Reverend, you mentioned yesterday that Simon had taken out substantial insurance coverage..."

He gave two or three big nods. "Oh, indeed. He took his duties as a husband and a father very seriously. Yes, he left Sylvie very well provided for."

"Were you aware of the size or nature of the coverage? Was it, for example, something that he or she ever discussed with you?"

His face went a little pale. He stared at Dehan and then turned back to me. "Am I to understand, Detectives, that I am a suspect in your investigation?"

I smiled and took a moment to answer. "These are routine questions, Reverend. We are trying to arrive at the truth, and sometimes that means asking innocent people questions that might sound offensive." I sat forward and leaned my elbows on the table next to Dehan's. "So, *were* you aware of the insurance coverage he had taken out for her?"

He shook his head, frowning. "No, we never discussed anything of the sort. I became aware of it after he had died. Speaking about finances makes me uncomfortable and he knew that."

I pressed him. "I assume you helped her to sort out all the details..."

"Naturally, Detective, we all did. We *are* a Christian community..."

Dehan grunted. "Did Sylvie know about the insurance?"

His frown deepened. "How could I possibly know that, Detective?"

I scratched my chin. "At what time did you leave for the Cavendishes' that afternoon?"

"I don't recall." He laughed. "It was almost twenty years ago! But if we were due to dine at seven or seven thirty, then I imagine I would have left at five or five thirty."

"Sure. You drove?"

"Almost certainly."

"Reverend, what is the nature of the relationship between yourself and Sylvie?"

"I *beg* your pardon?" His eyes were bright with anger.

I frowned at him, like he didn't make sense to me. I said, "It is a very simple question, Reverend. I don't know why it should cause offense. I am asking if you and Sylvie are intimate. What is the precise nature of your relationship?"

"We most certainly are *not* intimate! I am her pastor and her friend, no more!"

Dehan was watching him intently. She interrupted him. "What is it about that question that causes you offense, Reverend? As far as I am aware, Methodist pastors can marry . . ."

"Naturally, we can . . ."

"So a relationship with an attractive, available woman like Sylvie is perfectly feasible . . ."

"Well, yes, but I mean to say! That is not the nature of our relationship! What you are implying is appalling!"

I raised an eyebrow. "That you colluded? That you were accomplices?"

"How can you even imagine such a thing! I have devoted my entire life to helping people in the service of God. And she . . . well, she is as close to being angelic as any woman can be!"

Dehan raised her eyebrows high on her forehead. "Wow! That is high praise indeed."

He took a deep breath. His cheeks were flushed. "I have

perhaps expressed myself too forcefully. I must say I do not take it kindly that I came here in good faith to offer information and you have ambushed me into giving you an entirely erroneous impression. I have great admiration for Sylvie, but nothing more. If there had been any more, you may be sure we would have acted on it by now."

I made a face like I understood him and regretted our questions. "A murder investigation is not a pretty thing, Reverend. At the moment, nobody is a suspect, and everybody is. That's just the way it goes. We are grateful for your cooperation, but listen, just before you go. I wanted to ask you about Humberto . . ."

I watched his face really carefully. It did a lot of things. He blinked a few times. He frowned and his eyes narrowed. His lips contracted a few times like he was about to say something, but thought better of it. Finally, he said, "What about him? You surely can't suspect him!"

I grinned. "I refer you to my previous answer. What's his story? Where is he from? What is that language he speaks? Rumor has it you adopted him. Is that true?"

"No, it is not true. I did not adopt him. Rumor is just another word for gossip, Detective, and it is best to be ignored."

Dehan snorted. "Unless you're a cop. Then you find the subject of the gossip and you ask them to clarify the rumor. We call it following up on a lead."

He studied her face a minute, then looked back at me. "The way he speaks is called idioglossia. It is a form of language which he has created himself, out of Latin, especially liturgical Latin, Spanish, Portuguese, and a wide smattering of neologies, created by himself on a broad Latin base."

"What has caused him to create a language based entirely on Latin languages, with no English at all?"

He shook his head. "I have no way of answering your questions, Detective. Have they any relevance at all to your investigation, or are they merely the product of unseemly curiosity?"

"I won't know that," I said, "until I get the answers."

He looked me straight in the eye. "I can assure you that Humberto is the gentlest, kindest person you are ever likely to encounter, and he is incapable of causing harm, even to an insect at that."

I nodded. "No doubt you are right, Reverend. Thank you for coming in and giving us your information. We really appreciate it."

He stood, gave me a look that said he'd think twice before volunteering to help the cops in the future, nodded at Dehan, and left without shaking my hand.

"I think he's upset," she said to her fingers as she drummed them on the Formica tabletop. "I think he wanted a smiley sticker for having been a good boy."

"You are a heartless, mocking kind of girl, Dehan."

"Let's go to Eastchester, Stone, and call upon the Cavendishes." She looked up at me without smiling. "I've heard they do provide the most splendid alibis. Simply to *die* for!"

It took about twenty minutes to get to Country Club. The Cavendishes had their house right on the shore, on Country Club Road. It was a big, sprawling, terra-cotta affair with a double-entrance drive. I parked my Jag next to their Buick and Dehan rang the doorbell. The door was blond wood with stained glass panels. I noticed Dehan looking at them and sucking her teeth.

"What's the matter? You don't like the stained glass?"

"You telling me that's art? You disappoint me. I'll give you twenty bucks if that was made a day before 1973."

I heard the flap of Havaianas, and the door opened onto a woman who had been attractive a decade earlier and thought she still was, despite her sustained efforts at systematic self-destruction. All of this you could read in the mocking regard of her watery, slightly oversize eyes, and the way she held her gin and tonic as though it were an extension of her hand. Her jeans were too tight and her skin was too loose.

"My God, you look the part," she said. Dehan's eyebrows slid toward her hairline, and I pulled out my badge. I was about to speak, but she said, "I know who you are. Paul told me to expect you. Come in, the name's Liz, and for God's sake, loosen up and have a drink. Or a joint. You want a joint?"

I said, "Thanks, I've already eaten." But she turned and walked away from us. Dehan followed, and I stepped in and closed the door. We followed her voice, which called to tell us she was by the pool.

We found her sitting in a large wicker chair by a garden table, on a patio by a manicured lawn. The pool was some thirty feet away, shining a luminous turquoise with liquid, silver streaks. She pointed languidly to a trolley of drinks and said, "Make free. Is the sun over the yardarm yet, Detective Stone? Or am I being a very naughty girl?" She leered at Dehan. "You won't object if he uses his handcuffs on me, will you, Detective Dehan?"

We sat and I leaned on the table. It was barely midday and I already felt exhausted. "How many of those babies have you had, Mrs. Cavendish?"

She rolled her eyes. "Oh, you sound like my mother! What's it to you? There's no law . . ."

I sighed and interrupted her. "I don't give a damn how many you've had, Mrs. Cavendish. You can drink yourself into oblivion, for all I care. But I am here to check on Reverend Truelove's alibi, and if you are too drunk to be coherent, then we are all wasting our time. If you're drunk, we'll leave. If it's an act, cut it out."

Her cheeks flushed. She had large brown sunglasses perched on the top of her head, which she now lowered over her eyes and looked away.

"How rude," she said. "This is my first of the day, in fact."

"Good. I need to ask you about the night of the fifth of September, 1999. Now, I know it's a long time ago, but it's important that you be very accurate. If you are not sure, it is better that you tell us, rather than lie."

"I remember," she said, still staring at the pool. "Paul came to dinner that night."

"How can you be so sure?"

"Because the next morning he telephoned to tell me about poor Sylvie. Such a sad girl."

Dehan lifted her aviator shades onto the top of her head, in a strange echo of Liz Cavendish's recent and opposite movement. She narrowed her eyes and asked, "He phoned you in the morning? Can you remember what time that was?"

Mrs. Cavendish shrugged. "God, I don't know. I was still in bed, I remember that much. It must have been nine or ten at the latest."

There was something that wasn't squaring up for me. "How do you know Reverend Truelove, Mrs. Cavendish? Forgive me for being blunt, but you don't strike me as the Bronx Methodist Community type."

She finally looked at me and gave an ironic smile. "Finally, a compliment. Paul and I go back a very long way. We've been friends for decades. I met him in Brazil over thirty years ago, in the mid-eighties. He was half a ton of trouble back then, I can tell you that for free."

"Care to elaborate?"

"Not really."

I sighed. "Is Mr. Cavendish at home? We would like to talk to him as well."

She snorted. "Reggie? Reggie is *always* at home. He never leaves."

Dehan leaned forward. "Mrs. Cavendish, perhaps we haven't been clear enough with you. See, here's our problem. This is a murder investigation, and we have a very small pool of suspects. So that means that these people's alibis are really important. Because if the alibi doesn't hold up, or is unconvincing, that person could go to prison for twenty or thirty years. Which I figure would bring Reverend Truelove to somewhere around eighty-five or ninety before he joined you for a dinner party again. We are trying to discuss something important with you, Mrs. Cavendish. And the frivolous act isn't helping anyone, least of all your pal Paul."

She gave Dehan a look that was long and hostile. "My husband is paralyzed from the neck down. He also has brain damage. Forgive me if I seem frivolous, Detective. It's how I cope."

I asked, "How long has he been in this condition?"

"Twenty-five years. It's the reason we came back from Brazil. It was an accident, white water rafting."

"Was Reverend Truelove already back in the States?"

She took a long time to answer. "We all came back at roughly the same time."

"So, when he said that he was dining with 'the Cavendishes,' what he actually meant was that he was dining with you."

"Yes, Detective, that is what he meant. You have unearthed our sordid little secret." She heaved a big sigh. "Don't worry, I am not deluding myself. I know there are others. I told you, he was a ton of trouble back then and probably still is. Even if he has become insufferably pompous, there is no doubt he's shagging the brains out of this poor Sylvie woman too."

Dehan was in like a shot. "What makes you say that?"

"Sweetheart, because he would shag the table if he could find the right hole. And for some reason that only God understands, all those sweet, beatific Christian women just can't seem to keep their pure, lily-white legs together when that almighty, bombastic, pompous ass, the Great Reverend Paul Truelove, bestows one of his sainted smiles on them."

"He's a rake."

"That's another way of putting it, yeah. He's a fucking rake."

We sat for a moment in silence. Finally, I said, "Mrs. Cavendish, is there anything of what you've just said that you would like to change?"

"No."

"You are certain that Reverend Truelove was here on the night of the fifth of September, 1999."

"Yes."

"Then we won't take up any more of your time."

We stood but she didn't look at us. She just said, "See your-selves out, will you? And close the damn door while you are at it."

FIVE

I NEEDED TO THINK, SO INSTEAD OF GOING BACK TO THE precinct, I drove a mile or so north to the Huntington Woods, at Pelham Bay Park. We left the car in the parking lot and walked down through the trees to sit on the grass by the water.

It was almost midday, but the sun was already beginning to slip toward the south, giving its light a russet hue, making the shadows longer and the small waves look colder. I sat on an old, decaying wall, but Dehan walked on, down onto the mud, leaving deep imprints in the sludge. She had her hands in her back pockets, and the wind out of the south was making a mess of her long, black hair. She looked at the water for a long time, and then turned to face me. The lenses of her shades were like two copper suns. She made her way back toward me with slow, trudging steps, tying her hair in a knot behind her neck as she walked.

When she was a few feet away, she raised her voice over the wind. "His alibi isn't worth a thimble of piss."

I laughed. "That all depends on how good she is at giving evidence."

"They are lovers."

"They were lovers, we don't know if they still are."

She climbed up from the mud onto the blacktop and stood

stamping the mud from her boots. "Do you believe he was with her that night?"

"I have no idea."

"My gut tells me he called her last night and set it up. Why does a guy set up a false alibi?"

"Being guilty is only one possible reason. Another is that he is scared he is going to look guilty."

"You don't think he did it?"

I shook my head. "No, Ritoo Glasshopper. I think there is a damned good chance he did do it, but I just don't know why exactly. I am trying to listen to what the evidence is telling me. And . . ." I sighed. "At the moment, it is just burbling meaningless nonsense about Brazil. They were all out in Brazil together. Reggie broke his neck and they all came back to the Big Apple together. Reggie and Liz to their place on Eastchester Bay, and Paul screwing his parishioners in the East Bronx. Clearly, Dehan, there is more to this than meets the eye."

"What do you want to do now?"

I thought about it for a moment. "I would like to have another chat with Sylvie, without Reverend Truelove breathing down our necks. I would like to hear what she has to say about the reverend's being there or not during that day and the next morning. Also, though Sylvie's memory may be failing her, there is somebody else who was there whose memory may be a lot more reliable."

"Ahmed the gardener."

"Indeed." I stood. "Okay, let's go."

As we walked back toward the car, Dehan walked behind me, smacking my ass. I looked at her with scandalized eyes. "What the hell are you doing?"

"You have sand on your ass. You can't interview a witness with sand on your ass. It's not dignified."

. . .

THIS TIME, we found Sylvie at home. She opened the door like she was going to give it a spanking. She was wearing an apron and had her hair tied behind her head with a sock. When she saw who it was, she kind of sagged and said, "Oh, Detectives, I am kind of busy . . ."

Dehan smiled, not unkindly, and said, "You working?"

Sylvie nodded and gestured behind her for us to see. There was a mop in a bucket stenciled in the kitchen door and we could hear the washing machine churning its way through a cycle. Dehan nodded her understanding and said, "Yeah, so are we."

Sylvie had the good grace to smile as she sighed and stood back to let us in. "Sure, sorry. I get kind of caught up. Will you have some coffee?"

Dehan was doing fine, so I let her answer for us both. "Yeah, that would be nice. Thanks. We won't keep you long, Sylvie. Just a couple of quick questions."

Dehan followed her into the kitchen. I closed the door and stood looking a moment at the stairs that led up to the bedrooms. I wondered which stair she had been sitting on, and looked down at the carpet under my feet. It was kind of a pale beige. It was not the same one he had died on. I could see in my mind the crime scene photographs, the spot where he had lain, with his briefcase by his hand, so important to him in life, yet oddly irrelevant in death. Death has a way of radically altering essential values.

I became aware of their silhouettes framing the mop in the kitchen portal, watching me. I followed after them.

She had a kitchen of the sort that was known in the 1980s as "stripped pine pajamas." There was a big pine table in the middle of the floor and a large, no-nonsense AGA near a window that overlooked her back garden. Dehan sat at the table while Sylvie put on the coffee and I looked out the window. I could see the roof and fat tower of the church over the tops of the fruit trees and the hedge that separated her place from the plot where they had held the fête the day before.

I turned toward her. She was getting down a tin of brownies

from a cupboard. "It must be very convenient, having the church right at the back of your property like that."

She smiled. "It is."

"I'm surprised you haven't put a gate in the hedge."

She glanced at me. "I have thought about it, but it might be presuming a little too much."

I sat as she put the tin on the table and poured the coffee. "We have just come from visiting Elizabeth Cavendish."

"Gosh! I haven't seen Elizabeth for years. She used to visit quite regularly. She was a friend of Paul's. What has she got to do with your investigation?"

I gave my head a little "gee-gosh" sideways twitch and reached for a brownie. "In cold cases, we have to cast our nets wide." I watched her face carefully as I added, "Reverend Truelove was visiting them on the night of the crime."

She frowned. "Was he? My memory of that day is so hazy. I know he had been here earlier . . ."

Dehan dunked her brownie and bit into it. "Why's that?"

"We'd been talking about Ahmed, what days he would be at the church and what days with us. It wasn't difficult. He only had to come through . . ."

She faltered.

I prompted, "Yes? He only had to come through the hedge?"

She smiled. "It was easier in those days. It hadn't grown so thick."

Dehan frowned. "Forgive me, Sylvie, but it seems like a kind of odd thing to remember for almost twenty years."

Her eyes became abstracted. She looked unhappy. "It's an odd thing. The essential details are completely obliterated, yet small, trivial details seem to stand out so vividly. I can't explain it."

"It is very common, Sylvie," I said. "Trauma can play havoc with our memories. Have you seen a therapist?"

"I have the best therapist of all, Detective Stone. God is my therapist."

"Of course."

Dehan raised an eyebrow at her brownie, like she didn't believe something it had just whispered to her. "Sylvie, there is something we have been wanting to ask you. Please don't take this the wrong way. These are questions we are required to ask."

Her smile was oddly kind when she answered. "I do understand, Detective. And I can see how I would be a suspect. Please ask everything you need to. The truth is always our best defense."

"If only all witnesses took that view. Were you aware of the insurance policies that Simon had taken out in your favor, before he was killed?"

She shook her head. "No, he never discussed that kind of thing with me. He was real old-fashioned about the family finances and whatnot." She gave a small, pretty laugh. "He saw himself as a patriarch in the style of Abraham. We depended on him, and he provided." The smile faded. "Even in death, he faithfully provided."

Dehan nodded. "Sure, I get that. Would he have discussed matters like that with Reverend Truelove?"

"Oh, Lord no!" She laughed again. "Simon did not approve of Paul, at all. He accepted him because it was God's will. But he did not approve of him."

I sipped my coffee. "What caused his disapproval, Sylvie?"

There was no mistaking the look in her eyes as she gazed out the window toward the church. Whatever Simon may have thought, she definitely approved of the reverend.

"Paul doesn't always go by the book. He goes more by the spirit of the scriptures than by the letter. I guess he has faith in the guidance of the Lord, and that gives him courage to act on impulse. Simon went much more by the letter of the scriptures. I sometimes felt that he was afraid."

"Afraid of what?"

"Afraid of transgressing against the Word. He never did. And yet . . ." She turned and stared at me. "Do you think that evil can grow in a repressed heart, Detective?"

"What do you mean?"

She heaved a big sigh. "Is it possible that Paul's heart, though less tied to the letter of God's law, was also less repressed, and so had more room for kindness and humanity? While Simon's, through being so vigilant, so dogmatic, had become a repressed, dark place, with no room for forgiveness or compassion. And in the end he was struck down, like the Tower of Babel, for trying to get too close to God . . ."

I made a thinking noise, wondering at what point it had stopped being a question and become a statement. "I am not sure if you are asking me or telling me, Sylvie. Either way, I think it's a question I am not qualified to answer. What I am pretty sure of, though, is that Simon was not struck down by God, but by a human being. And I aim to find out who that is. As far as I can see, there are only two people who might have seen him. You, and possibly Ahmed. Have you still got Ahmed's contact details?"

She nodded, got to her feet, and moved over to a large pine dresser. She pulled an old phone book from a packed drawer and leafed through it. Then she copied down a number and an address onto a piece of paper and brought it over to me before sitting down again.

"He is no longer involved with the church. He returned to Islam."

I studied the piece of paper a moment and then put it in my pocket. "Sylvie, you said Reverend Truelove was here earlier in the day to discuss Ahmed's roster. What time would that have been around? Before lunch, after lunch . . . ?"

She gazed over at the church again. She looked distressed. "After. After lunch. They came over together and then Ahmed set to work on the fruit trees, the plums and the apples, collecting the harvest. And Paul and I talked and had coffee. Then he left, about six I guess. He had to go, to . . ."

She frowned.

"To what, Sylvie?"

"I don't recall." She gave a small laugh. "I suppose he had to get ready to go and have dinner with Elizabeth Cavendish."

I nodded. "No doubt."

I stood. Dehan was watching me with narrowed eyes. "Thank you, Sylvie. You have been very helpful."

Dehan stood and we left.

As we drove away, I could see Sylvie standing in the doorway, watching us.

SIX

DEHAN SAT WATCHING ME AND FROWNED. I GLANCED at her a couple of times as we moved from Pierce Avenue onto Bronxdale. All I could see was the street passing behind her head and my own reflection duplicated in her shades. Finally, she said, "There is something on your mind you are not sharing. What have I missed?"

I made a face. She was right. "I'm not sure. It may be nothing. I need to check it out first. I want you to contact the insurance company and find out if they have any correspondence on file between themselves and Sylvie from before the fifth of September, 1999. Let's see if she's telling the truth."

"Meanwhile . . . ?"

"I'm going to talk to Ahmed and see if his story tallies with hers."

"You think she's lying?"

I shrugged. "I don't know. The way she kept staring out the window at the church, I just got a hunch." I looked at her again. She was waiting. "I had the feeling she was remembering more than she was telling us about."

She nodded. "Yeah. I had that feeling too."

"When you're done with the insurance company, see if you

can get any information on Humberto. But I don't want the reverend to know we are looking. See if you can get a Social Security number or something. You know what to do."

"Sure."

"Then what do you say we get together for a beer this evening and compare notes? I'll buy you a steak at 900 Park."

She looked embarrassed. "I can't."

My face said I was surprised. "Oh?"

"My uncle has invited me to dinner at his house."

"Oh, sure. So we can catch up in the morning."

"Yeah. Well, anyway, I'll call you if anything important comes up."

"Sure." I smiled. "Likewise."

I DROPPED Dehan at the precinct and took White Plains Road north to Morris Park Avenue, then ducked left and right into Unionport Road, by the railway lines. It was a place designed according to the Who-Gives-a-Fuck school of architecture, by people who didn't care, for people they thought didn't matter. Ahmed had a gray, featureless two-story house with iron rails on the front door and the windows. There was a lot of shouting going on inside in a language I didn't understand, and there seemed to be men, women, and children involved. I rang the bell and wondered if they'd heard it over their massed voices.

Somebody had, because a small man in his midthirties opened the door after a while, dressed in a vest, pajama pants, and slippers. He had a couple of days' stubble and large, vaguely amused brown eyes. He said, "What?" but not in a hostile way.

I showed him my badge and told him who I was.

He took the badge and examined it. Then handed it back and shrugged. "What I can do for you?" He gestured with both hands into his house. "Everybody has got papers. We have a simple life. Why NYPD?"

"Are you Ahmed Abadi?"

"Yes. That me." He shrugged, spread his hands. "We simple family . . ."

"Cut the act, Ahmed. I know you've been here since you were a kid and I know your English is just fine. Can I come in? I need to talk to you."

He grinned. "Okay. What about? I keep my nose clean, Detective Stone."

"It is not about you, and it has nothing to do with immigration. You may have unwittingly been a witness in a crime a long time ago. I just need to ask you a couple of simple questions . . ." I paused. "Can I come in?"

He led me into a narrow hallway carpeted in an orange patterned fabric designed to give you chronic depression while simultaneously curing you with static electric shock treatment. He pushed into a cramped living room, hollering a stream of what sounded like obscenities. Two women in burkas and six kids of varying ages fled the room, giggling. He gestured with both hands at a sofa that was a mistake in the 1970s and was still a mistake today and said, "Please, sit, can I give you some tea?"

I sat. "No, thank you, Ahmed. This won't take long."

He did the whole shrugging and spreading his hands thing again, like I was missing out on a once-in-a-lifetime chance, and sat down, smiling with his eyes.

"How can I help you?"

"About eighteen years back, you used to work for Simon Martin, over on Bogart Avenue, and for the church that backed onto that house . . ."

"Reverend Paul Truelove. Very beautiful people; they were so kind and helpful to me when I was new in this country. I hold them always very close to my heart, Allah be merciful."

I nodded. "You probably remember that back then Simon Martin was the victim of a home invasion . . ."

His face had changed in a second and he looked like he might cry.

"It was a tragedy. I pray every day for his soul. Such a good man, with an equally as good wife, beautiful baby. Kind people. How can this happen to such a kind family? I want to know. How can this happen? Allah be merciful!"

"Well, that is what we are trying to find out. We have reopened the investigation, Ahmed, and as I understand it, you were there on the day in question, with Reverend Truelove."

He was doing big nods, involving his whole upper body. "I was. I was. You want to know what I saw, and what I remember?"

"That would be very helpful."

He sank back in his chair. His eyes became abstracted. "It is such long time ago. I was . . ." He shook his head, pulling down the corners of his mouth. "Fifteen? Sixteen? Just a boy." He gave a small laugh. "So grateful to be away from Iraq! So grateful for starting this new life! And to Paul and Simon . . ." He sighed, and I waited. "They were trying to decide what is best, I work for Paul Monday, Tuesday, Wednesday, and Simon Thursday, Friday, and Sunday?"

"Sunday. Not Saturday?"

"No, Sunday, because Saturday is bad for me. Sunday. Or maybe they think is best I work for Paul in the mornings and Simon after lunch. They were wondering, talking, talking. This day Simon is at work. He is *always* at work! Six, seven days of the week. I joke with him, 'If the week have fourteen days, Mr. Simon, you would work fourteen days!' He laugh a little . . ." He held his fingers together to show a really small amount. "He's a man who does no laugh much. 'We praise God in our work!' he say to me. I say, 'Allah be praised!'"

"So what happened this day?"

"Paul he say me, 'Come on! We go talk with Sylvie! She will decide!' so we go through the garden. Is very good. The gardens are connected so we can go, pom pom pom, through the garden to her house."

"What time would that have been around, can you remember?"

He rocked from side to side, like he was listening to a sweet melody. "Maybe five or six. I go always to Paul after four, five. So he go inside to have coffee and talk with Sylvie, and I start to collect fruit from the plum trees and the apple trees."

"What happened next?"

"I am working, pompompom, pompompom, and Paul come to the step of the kitchen door. He said to me, 'Ahmed!' And he put up his thumb." He showed me the thumbs-up gesture. "He say me, 'It is all set up, you work afternoons for Simon and Sylvie. Mornings with me.' I say him, 'Sounds good to me' and he go."

"What time?"

"Oh, it must be around six. Maybe more."

"What did you do with the fruit?"

He smiled. "Put in baskets and leave them in the kitchen. Sylvie tell me she is going to make jam and pies to sell for the church. She say maybe she will have some extra for me." He winked, and his grin was infectious. "She is very good woman. Very religious, with God. Allah is merciful. I clean the leaves, water the flowers, and I go."

"How did you go?"

"Through garden to church. Then I got on the bus."

"I want you to think very carefully about this question, Ahmed. It is very important. If you are not sure, then just say you are not sure, okay? Did you or Mrs. Martin close the kitchen door before you left?"

He put his hands over his eyes and then slid them slowly onto his forehead. His eyes were wide and abstracted. "No . . ." he said. "No, don't say this to me. I leave the door open. Is this how he is getting in? Oh, man . . . !"

I shook my head. "We don't know yet, Ahmed. Don't blame yourself. He might have got in any number of ways. You are sure you left the door open?"

"Yes."

"I know it's a long time ago, but anything you can remember is helpful. Did you happen to notice anybody or anything that struck you as odd, strange, out of place?"

He shrugged and sighed. "Maybe, then, but is such long time. I don't remember." He made a "pfff" sound. "And you know, it is Bronx, right? What is strange is when you don't see nothing strange."

"I hear you. Ahmed, you have been very helpful. Thank you." I stood, and he stood with me.

"We always want to help the police. Anything at all, we are here, you are always welcome." We shook hands and he saw me to the door. "Please, come again."

I made my way back to the Jag and sat thinking and turning things around in my head, and whichever way I turned them, I couldn't get them to sit right. It just didn't work, however I looked at it. At least one person was lying, and I was pretty sure it wasn't Ahmed.

I took my time driving back, running over every detail in my mind, trying to find the corners and the straight edges of the jigsaw, hoping I'd catch Dehan before she left for her uncle's.

I parked in the lot, crossed the road, and stepped into the lobby. Maria was behind the desk and gave me an insolent wink. "Hey, handsome!"

I raised an eyebrow at her. "Hello, Sergeant. Don't make me report you for sexual harassment."

"In your dreams, white boy!"

"You know about that? Listen, Detective Dehan here?"

"You just missed her. Her date picked her up about ten minutes ago."

I smiled. "Her date? That was her uncle."

Maria raised an eyebrow of her own to devastating effect. "That's her *uncle*? Well, I would sure love to see her cousin! This dude was no more than thirty-two, and fit! You know what I am sayin'? I ain't talkin' about his health! They went off in his Mercedes-Benz an' she didn't even say goodbye."

I felt odd. She must have seen it because she adopted a mother hen look. "Well, what do you expect, Stone? Girl with those looks! You don't do nothin' about it, you're gonna lose her!"

"Maria, what are you talking about?"

She pointed at me. "You wannit? You put a ring on it!"

"Keep your office gossip, and your fantasies, to yourself. I'll see you tomorrow."

"*Si, si* . . . Ha!"

I went and reported to the captain, then drove home, feeling inexplicably deflated.

SEVEN

NEXT MORNING, DEHAN CAME IN LATE AT NINE THIRTY, with bags under her eyes and a face like sour retribution. I waited till she had sat down before I looked at her.

"How was your date?" I asked mildly, looking back at the papers I was reading.

"It wasn't a date. I told you. It was my uncle."

"Mm-hm." I affected to be engrossed in the information I had printed out from the electoral register. "That would be the drop-dead-gorgeous thirty-year-old uncle with the Mercedes."

"What? You're spying on me now?"

I shrugged, still not looking at her. "To quote a dear friend of mine, 'We are partners, we should tell each other things.'"

"I never said anything that lame."

"Words to that effect. So who is the lucky guy?"

"Nobody."

"Suit yourself. I have been searching since six this morning and I can find no trace of Humberto, either as Truelove or any other name, at the reverend's address or any other address."

"Snap."

I frowned at her. "Snap?"

"That's what I was doing last night when I was abducted by aliens. You've been here since six?"

"I couldn't sleep."

"Yeah, you look like shit. You should have called me. I couldn't sleep either."

"I thought you might be otherwise engaged."

She gave me a look that would have curdled distilled water. "I'm alone when I lower my lamp, thanks, Sensei. Not that it's any of your damn business. Moving on, did you see the email from the insurance company?"

"Not yet," I said, feeling oddly cheerful all of a sudden. "What do they say?"

"You won't like it. It looks like your friend Sylvie, the girl next door, ain't so wholesome and mom's apple pie after all."

"Oh?"

She reached in a manila folder, pulled out two sheets of A4, and tossed them across the table at me. "February, 1999. Two emails, addressed to her, advising her of the insurance policies taken out in her favor by her husband."

I read through them. They were brief, to the point, and very clear.

"That doesn't look very good, does it?"

"How did you get on with Ahmed?"

I ran through the interview. She thought about it. "Pretty much confirms what she said, only in more detail."

I nodded. "Pretty much." I sighed. "You know what? The story . . ." I narrowed my eyes and shook my head, searching for the right words. "You hear it from Sylvie, you hear it from the reverend, you hear it from Ahmed, and you read it in the report, and it seems to be the same story . . ." I pointed at her. "Prima facie . . . but it doesn't quite jibe with me. The versions are slightly dissonant. The people who remember were not quite there, and the only person who *was* there, doesn't remember. And then there are the small 'mistakes,' half-truths and lies . . . I want to get Paul and Sylvie in an interrogation room and scare them half to death until they stop playing games and start coming clean."

Dehan was nodding. "Sure, they're pissing me off too."

I drummed the tabletop with my fingers for a moment. "Do you know, Dehan, what day of the week was the fifth of September, in 1999?"

She looked vaguely surprised. "You want me to check?"

"No. I know. I just wondered if you did."

"No. I'm not that kind of freak. I'm weird in other ways."

A flicker of a smile. I flickered back. "It was a Sunday."

She closed her eyes. "Man." She said it with a strange mixture of self-reprimand and genuine admiration. "You are good, Sensei. That is . . ." She opened her eyes and nodded. "What the fuck is a pastor doing dining out on a Sunday evening at seven p.m.?"

"I am no expert, but as I understand it, he should have been in mass, or whatever Methodists do instead. And when we were talking to Sylvie, she realized that. She was about to say that he went back to deliver the sermon and faltered. Between them, they are concocting lies, and I want to know why." I sat forward. "Tell you what, Carmen, why don't you get the phone records for Reverend Truelove for the fifth to the sixth of September, 1999, and let's see exactly when he did call her. Then maybe we get them both in here and have a talk."

"On it!"

While she did that, I continued searching for any trace of Humberto. There was none. As far as I could tell, he was not officially in the United States. He was not registered at the rectory of St. George's Church, nor could I find more than a handful of Humbertos in New York. Those I found were not him. Which only left one explanation.

I was half aware of the printer churning out documents, but ignored it and turned over the significance of that explanation in my mind. After a bit, I heard Dehan say, "Well, I'll be."

I looked at her. "You will?"

"He called her at nine thirty that night."

"For how long?"

"They talked for forty-five minutes." She stood and walked to the window. There she turned and rested her ass on the windowsill. She said, "He's a rake. That's been established, right?"

"I think so."

"Simon is a royal pain in the ass who thinks he's Abraham, but ain't. When he gets posted to New York, being a good patriarch, he takes out life insurance to protect his wife and daughter in case the children of Babylon should do for him. Only it wasn't the children of Babylon he needed to be worrying about.

"His wife receives an email informing her that her husband is now worth more dead than alive. At first, it doesn't even register. But then, when they get here and move into their house by the church, and she meets the fascinating and sexually magnetic Reverend Truelove, the insurance begins to take on a greater significance. What if . . . ?"

I nodded. "But she is incapable of doing it herself."

She raised a finger. "Shut up. As you say, she hasn't the strength, or the killer instinct, to do this by herself. Paul, however, is—how did Elizabeth Cavendish describe him? Half a ton of trouble? He is not constrained by the letter of Divine Law. He has warmth and humanity in his heart. So, they start to have an affair. She promises him that if he will get rid of Simon, she will be his and his only."

I frowned. "So how did they do it?"

"Shut up. He comes over with Ahmed, so he has a witness other than Sylvie to say that he left. After Ahmed has gone, perhaps during the reading from scripture by a lay member of the congregation, he slips back though the garden, kills Simon, and returns to the church as the reading of the scripture is concluded. Then he delivers his sermon, like he has been there all along."

We stared at each other for a while. It was something we did unconsciously which other people found disturbing, but it helped us to think. After a moment, I said, "It sounds a bit like the plot from an Agatha Christie novel."

"Okay, but . . . the bones . . ."

"It would require very precise timing."

She shook her head. "No. It would require approximate timing and a cell phone on vibrate."

I nodded. "She hears his car arriving. Calls the reverend. He invites John Doe to read the lesson and slips out. She has left the back door open for him. He comes in, knocks Simon down and kills him, gives her the phone to call 911, and races back to the church."

"See?"

I sighed. "It's crazy enough that it may have worked."

"And I am figuring that Paul Truelove is all about being crazy. Crazy in the Amazon, crazy at Eastchester Bay, and crazy in the Bronx."

I was quiet for a bit. It was hard to find fault with it, and like she said, it kind of fit with the picture of Paul Truelove that was beginning to emerge.

"What do you make of Humberto?"

"Have you been able to find him?"

"Nope. Nowhere. He is not officially in this country."

She made a "yeah, that's what I expected" face and said, "I have absolutely no reason for saying this, but I'm pretty sure you've had the same thought. I figure he's Truelove's son from a Brazilian affair."

"The thought had crossed my mind. I wouldn't be surprised if it had as much to do with his coming back to the U.S. as Reggie Cavendish's accident. What I can't decide is whether that has anything to do with this case, or whether it is just part of the general chaos and collateral damage associated with his life."

Dehan gave a small grunt. "In as much as he has probably left a string of heartbroken, pregnant parishioners in his wake, halfway around the globe."

I frowned. "So why didn't they get hitched afterwards? And what made this Don Juan of the Altar go to such lengths for Sylvie?"

She gave me a knowing look and wagged a finger at me. "Because . . . she never really wanted him. They probably never even slept together. She just wanted him to do the deed. And once he'd done it, she sold him the 'it's not you, it's me, I am too traumatized' line. And it was the fact that he could not have her that drove him to the extreme of killing for her."

I thought about it. It wasn't the strangest story I'd ever heard, not by a long shot. People will do some pretty crazy things when their hormones get stirred up. One thing was for sure. He had lied about being at Elizabeth Cavendish's house. He had been in the right place at the right time to kill Simon Martin, and both Elizabeth and Sylvie had backed him up in that lie.

I nodded. "I think it's time to rattle their cages. You get Sylvie, I will go get Paul." I stood and paused a moment. "Dehan, be totally unsympathetic. She'll break down and start crying. When she does, do nothing. Let's see what happens next."

"Gotcha. What about the reverend?"

"I'm going to tell him that Sylvie and Elizabeth have sold him out. We'll play it by ear and maybe we can play them against each other."

As we moved toward the door, I said, "You got your car, right?"

"Yeah, you didn't pick me up this morning. Remember?"

"I didn't want to disturb . . ."

"Asshole."

I watched her walk down the sidewalk toward her car, on her long, beautiful legs, and smiled to myself.

EIGHT

I PULLED UP IN FRONT OF THE CHURCH AND WAS surprised to see Dehan pull up on the other side of the street. I'd expected her to continue on to Bogart Avenue to get Sylvie. I climbed out of the Jag and waited for her to join me. She spoke as she approached.

"I had a hunch. I called ahead and spoke to Mary. As I thought, Sylvie is at the church."

"This should make things interesting."

We entered the grounds and climbed the steps to the big red door. Our shadows, elongated by the early autumn sun, lay warped across the stone flags. We paused and listened. Hushed voices seemed to slide and roll up the walls and into the cavernous arches of the ceiling. I touched Dehan's shoulder and pointed. The reverend and Sylvie stood at the door of the vestry in close, quiet conversation. I couldn't make out the words, but whatever it was they were talking about seemed important, even urgent.

I moved quietly into the side aisle and walked toward them with Dehan just behind me. They sensed the movement and turned. His face was serious. He sighed very loudly.

"Detectives! This is becoming . . ." He let the words hang.

"Would it not be better to deal with all of your questions in one go, and be done with it?"

He labored the last four words so that they resounded against the thick stone walls, like the end of an impactful sermon.

"It would," I said. "That's why we are here. We would like you and Mrs. Martin to come with us to the precinct. There are a couple of issues which . . ." I paused and shook my head. "Well, however Detective Dehan and I look at them, we just can't make them square up."

His expression was impatient. "It is very inconvenient. I have work to do, so does Sylvie. Really, Detective Stone, we have been more than patient and accommodating, but sincerely, this is bordering on . . ."

"Patient and accommodating?" I said it without any particular inflection.

He frowned. "Well, yes . . ."

"We are investigating the murder of one of your parishioners and, as I understand it, a friend of yours." I turned to Sylvie. "Your husband and the father of your daughter. I'm struggling to see where patience and accommodation come into it."

He closed his eyes and heaved another sigh. She looked down and fiddled with her thumb. He said, "The investigation was dropped eighteen years ago, Detective. We did not ask for it to be reopened. We have all . . . moved on!"

I ignored him. "Will you both please accompany us to the station?"

The reverend's face flushed. "Have we any choice?"

Dehan nodded. "Sure. You can refuse. But I wouldn't recommend it, because then we can either arrest you on suspicion of murder or take you into custody as material witnesses. So maybe the best thing is to cooperate with us. I am assuming, Reverend, that we want the same thing here, to catch the person who murdered Mr. Martin. Am I wrong?"

Sylvie answered. "Of course you are not wrong. It's just very painful to revisit all this stuff, just as we were . . ."

There was a scuff and a footfall behind us. I turned to look. Humberto was standing silhouetted in the glare from the doorway. His voice was almost a whisper, but it carried, reverberating against the high stone walls.

"*Donna . . . Donna Maria plena di graza . . .*"

Reverend Truelove glanced at him and then waved him away. "It's all right, Humberto. Go back to your room. Everything is fine."

Humberto reached out his left hand toward us. The fingers of his right went to his large lower lip. "*Venite, Donna. Venite com migo. Ven . . .*"

Sylvie smiled. It was a sad expression. She shook her head. "I can't come now, Humberto. I have to go with these people."

He must have picked up something in the tone of her voice, or in our demeanor. Whatever it was, he knew something was wrong and let out a deep, guttural noise that seemed to come from down in his belly. He pouted his thick lips and shook his huge head.

"No . . . *No* . . . *Noooo* . . ."

It was like a tantrum coming on in a four-year-old, only Humberto was well over six feet and must have weighed well over two hundred and sixty pounds. Reverend Truelove scowled at us. "Excuse me." He moved toward Humberto, reaching out for him with both arms. "Humberto, come. Go back to your room . . ."

The noise Humberto let out then was horrific. It was like a wounded grizzly roaring at the mountains. It reverberated from the rafters down to the stone flags and bounced off the walls, filling every corner of the church. It was not a word, but an inarticulate cry of immoderate, irrational pain. He stamped his huge feet and his arms started flapping as the reverend tried to take hold of him, and next thing, he was bellowing at the top of his voice, "*El Diavolo! Malefico! Malefico! El Diavolo e la Diavola! Malefica! Malefica! None llevare! E la mia donna!*"

The reverend struggled to keep Humberto's arms down and block his way, but his size and strength made it hard, and

Humberto kind of plowed through him, driving him back as he pushed toward Sylvie. A spasm of grief flashed across her face and she stepped toward him.

"Humberto. It's all right, honey! These are friends." She hurried around the pews and made her way down the central aisle, reaching for him.

Humberto pushed the reverend aside and enfolded Sylvie in his arms. "*Donna! Donna Maria plena di graza! Diavolo malefico! Diavola! Diavola malefica! None llevare. E la mia donna!*"

His face had folded up like it had melted in the heat of the sun, and now he had tears streaming down his face. Sylvie looked small and fragile in his massive arms. He'd gone quiet, except for a few shuddering sobs, and she was soothing him, whispering to him that we were just friends.

We joined them. The reverend was looking uncomfortable. I studied his face a moment. "You got somebody who can look after him for a couple of hours?"

He nodded. "If you can give us a few minutes, we'll take him to my housekeeper." He turned to Sylvie. "And maybe we could prevail upon Mary . . ."

Sylvie nodded, then pulled back and held Humberto's face in her hands. "Hey, you want to see Mary?"

He grinned all over his wet face. His breath shuddered as he nodded. Dehan was already on the phone.

"Mary? This is Detective Dehan. Listen, can you join us in the church? We need somebody to look after Humberto for a couple of hours . . . Thanks." She hung up and glanced at Sylvie. "She's coming."

Fifteen minutes later, Mary had managed to coax Humberto away to the rectory, with promises of hot chocolate and cake, and we led the reverend and Sylvie out to the cars. But when Sylvie saw that Dehan was taking her across the road, and I was taking the reverend toward my Jag, she stopped dead in her tracks on the sidewalk and refused to move. A spasm of panic constricted her face, giving her the look of a terrified child.

"What's going on? Why are you separating us? Why do I have to go on my own?"

I studied her face, trying to read her reaction and what it meant.

"We want to get this over with as much as you do, Sylvie. Detective Dehan is going to ask you some questions, and I am going to talk to Reverend Truelove for a bit. It saves time that way, and we can all go home and get on with our lives."

She turned terrified eyes on the reverend. He nodded and said, "Let's get it over with, Sylvie."

She hesitated and then followed Dehan to her car.

I let Dehan get ahead and drove at a leisurely pace. The reverend was quiet, staring out the side window at the anonymous, fleeting people on the sunlit sidewalks. "I cannot believe," he said without looking at me, "that you seriously consider Sylvie a suspect in this case."

"Who says we do?"

Now he turned to me. "Come on! You were about to arrest her in there!"

"Was I?"

"Well, that is what your partner said."

"That was one of a number of options she put to both of you."

He was silent for a moment. "So I am the suspect and she is the material witness . . ."

"Nothing says 'guilty' like a stupid lie, Reverend. And you would do well to remember that during the interview when we get to the station."

He sighed, closed his eyes, and flopped back in his seat. He didn't talk again until we arrived at the precinct.

NINE

I SAT OPPOSITE HIM AND PLACED A THIN MANILA folder in front of me. He glanced at it and then up at my face. I stared at him a moment, and when I was sure I had his full attention, I said, "I spoke to Elizabeth Cavendish. She confirmed your alibi."

He swallowed. "My alibi . . ."

"Yes. Your alibi. She also mentioned that her husband has been paralyzed from the neck down for the last twenty-five years."

He wouldn't make eye contact and his breathing rate had increased noticeably. "Yes, that was a tragic accident."

"Where did it happen?"

"In Brazil."

"Was that where Humberto was conceived?"

Now he met my eye. "How is that relevant to your investigation?"

"I don't know."

"Then let's leave it."

"Okay, fine. What is the relationship between you and Elizabeth Cavendish?"

His face flushed. "We are friends."

"Close friends?"

"Yes, we go back a long way."

"How intimate is your friendship?"

His anger was explosive, but it looked to me like he was using it to hide his fear. "Really, Detective! This is too much!"

"What is, Reverend? The suggestion that you and she are having an affair is that infuriating? I don't see that that's too much at all."

He spluttered. "She's a married woman!"

"She is a very frustrated, comparatively young woman, with emotional and sexual needs, who is married to a man who cannot fulfill those desires. You are both close and she is clearly drawn to you. Tell me where it becomes too much."

He was foundering, trying to find a firm footing somewhere. "Naturally, I have been there for her! But as a friend, nothing more . . ."

"She said you were lovers. Was she lying?"

He gasped.

I repeated, "Was she lying?"

He hesitated and then hesitated some more. He was screwed whichever way he went and he knew it. Finally, he said, "No," and sagged. "That is, we *were* lovers. Years ago, for a very brief period of time. We had a short, ill-advised affair after her husband's accident."

"You are not lovers now?"

"No."

"How many lovers have you had, Reverend?"

"That is none of your *damned* business!"

"I disagree."

"How . . . ?"

"Liz says you are, and I quote, 'a rake.'" It was Dehan who'd said it, but Elizabeth had agreed and not retracted her statement.

"Well, I . . . ! That may be her opinion, but it is certainly not the truth! I am a man of God, Detective!"

"Is she lying?"

He heaved another sigh to steady his nerves. "Look, Detective, you are trying to make me say she is a liar, because in doing so I will undermine my own 'alibi,' as you call it. But I am not going to call her a liar because she is not a liar. She may see me as a rake for reasons of wounded pride, loneliness, or any number of reasons. But that is her subjective view, and I can assure you it is not based on any factual information. I am *not* a rake!"

"What is the nature of your relationship with Sylvie Martin?"

His face went like stone. "I have already told you, I am her pastor. We are friends. And that is all, honest truth."

"What time did you go to Elizabeth Cavendish's house that night?"

He spread his hands and shook his head. "You are asking me for details of something that happened twenty years ago. I suppose about six o'clock, perhaps a little earlier. Traffic is heavy at that time of night."

I nodded and smiled, one New Yorker to another. "You're not kidding."

He smiled back, a hint of relief on his face.

I said, "Now here's the problem, Paul." His eyebrows twitched at the use of his first name. He had lost his title and that worried him even more. "Can you remember what you did earlier that day?"

"Of course not."

"You took Ahmed over to Sylvie's house, to discuss what days and times he would work at the church, and when he would work for her and Simon."

He shrugged. "Did I? Yes, that's very possible. But I fail to see . . ."

"Ahmed came over to the rectory after five. You chatted. Then you went over to Sylvie's house, and while he collected the plums and the apples from the trees at the end of the garden, you and Sylvie sat and had coffee, and discussed his hours."

"Clearly you think this is important . . ."

"It is important, because you left Sylvie's house just after six. And there is no way you had time to get from there to Country Club in time for dinner. Which means that you and Elizabeth have concocted a false alibi . . ."

"Now wait just one minute!"

". . . which also makes me wonder, what would make you do that?"

"You are leaping to wild, unwarranted conclusions!"

"I don't see how."

"If I was not there, then it is a genuine mistake . . ."

"You said you discovered the next morning what had happened. That is not the kind of thing you suddenly forget."

"Well, I . . . It is a long time ago, Detective!"

"But quite a memorable event, wouldn't you say? So were you there for her, or not? And if not, why not?"

He started to speak three times, and three times stopped himself. Then, he went for it and decided to brazen it out. "No! I am certain that I was dining with Liz! Ahmed and Sylvie must be mistaken."

I shrugged like it wasn't important. "You may be right. I just thought I'd better check. Moving on to another matter. What is the norm in Methodist churches, Reverend, regarding Sunday Mass, as compared, for example, with the Catholic Church?"

He visibly relaxed and breathed more deeply. "Well, we are somewhat more flexible than our Roman friends." He smiled as though he'd said something funny. "It varies from church to church. For my part, in the summer we worship in the morning on Sundays to allow people to relax in the afternoon and evening before starting the week. However, in the fall and in the winter, a lot of people find comfort in evening worship. So, as of the first Sunday in September, we meet for prayers and a reading of Scripture on Sunday evenings at about seven. Until the last Sunday in April."

I nodded and smiled. "That pretty much fits with my research. Have you always followed that regime?"

"Always. Why?"

"September the fifth, 1999, was a Sunday."

He closed his eyes. Then, after a moment, he buried his face in his hands.

I went on, "You have lied to me consistently and systematically since you first opened your mouth to me. And you are so damned arrogant and stupid that every time I catch you in a lie, you just keep lying more. Now, I told you in the car, nothing says 'guilty' like a stupid lie. So right now, you have managed to lie your way right to the top of my list of suspects. You have a big sign nailed to your two-inch brow that says, 'I'm the Guy.'" I sat forward and said, "Look at me." He removed his hands from his face. I held my forefinger and thumb in front of him, an eighth of an inch apart. "I am this close to arresting you and charging you with Simon's murder."

"No! *No! No! No!* You have it all *wrong!*"

"If—*if!*—I have it all wrong, it is because you keep telling me half-assed stupid lies that a four-year-old could see through. Now, keep bullshitting me, Reverend, and you and Humberto . . ."

"*No!*"

"*. . . get fast-tracked to Attica!*"

Our voices clashed, then died away and left a ringing silence. I pointed at him. "Think about it. I'm going to talk to Sylvie. When I get back, I want to hear the truth. If I get more lies, I will charge you and start building my case with the DA. I have means, opportunity, and motive."

"What motive?"

"The oldest two in the book. Your love for Sylvie and your desire to get your hands on her house, including her recently deceased husband's life insurance. And I have a string of lies long enough to convince any jury that whatever you say, they should believe the opposite." I stood. "Now, if it don't work, stop doing it! I have warned you."

I stepped out into the corridor, grabbed some black,

caffeinated coffee from the machine, and pushed into interview room two, where Dehan was talking to Sylvie.

Dehan was saying, "Now, see, Sylvie, here is the part I'm having some difficulty with. You are telling me that the reverend left you at around six, while Ahmed was working in the garden, to go to have dinner with Elizabeth Cavendish . . ."

Sylvie looked pale and drawn. "I don't know if that's what he did. I assume that's what he did if that is what he says."

"You think he might be lying?"

"No!"

I said, "Have you ever known the reverend to lie?"

"No! Of course not!"

"So you think he did go to Elizabeth's house?"

"If that's what he says he did, yes."

"So the problem I have," Dehan pressed on, "is that there is no way he could have gotten to Elizabeth's house on time if he left you after six."

She spread her hands. "Perhaps he arrived late."

"No. According to Elizabeth, he was not late."

"I don't know what you want me to say."

I leaned forward. "You see, there is something else, and I think you know this already. The day Simon was killed was a Sunday, the first Sunday in September, and there was a service at the church. So there was no way he could have been dining with Elizabeth Cavendish."

"He must have made a mistake."

"Why wasn't he there for you the night your husband was murdered, Sylvie? If he was not out, if he was at the church, why was he not there for you?"

"He was! He would have been! I don't remember!"

Dehan was shaking her head. "No. I think you do remember, Sylvie. I think you remember very well. And I think you were right the first time. He was there. He was there for you every step of the way."

"What do you mean?"

Dehan changed tack. "Why did he lie to us about being at Elizabeth's?"

"I don't know!"

"So he did lie!"

"No! I don't know! *No!*"

"He wasn't there. He was at the church, delivering a sermon. He knew it and you knew it. Why did he say he was with Elizabeth and persuade her to lie for him? What *really* happened that night, Sylvie?"

Her face was crimson, she had tears in her eyes, and she was almost hysterical. "I don't know! I don't remember!"

"When did you hear from him? When did he contact you?"

She was sobbing, with her face in her hands. "The next morning, I think. I don't remember."

"Not that night?"

"No! I keep telling you. I don't remember, I am not sure."

I spoke quietly. "Okay, Sylvie, take it easy. Let's talk about something you do remember. When was the first time you discovered that your husband had taken out life insurance to safeguard you and Mary?"

She wiped her face and looked at me with pleading eyes. "You asked me this already. I told you, after he died."

Dehan said, "But we have copies of emails sent to you by the insurance company in February of 1999 advising you that you have been named the beneficiary in two insurance policies, and detailing the amount of the coverage."

She looked bewildered. "What?"

Dehan slipped them out of her folder and slid them across the table. Sylvie looked at them and shook her head. "Even if I had received these, I would not have read them."

Dehan frowned. "Why?"

"I would have left them for Simon to read. He took care of anything like that."

"He had access to your email?"

"Access? It wasn't *my* email! It was our email!"

I shook my head. "I am sorry, Sylvie. There is not a jury in this country that is going to believe that."

I said it, but I knew I was wrong. She began to cry again.

"I *swear* to you. I had no idea about that insurance. I have no idea where Paul was, or why he seems to have lied to you. I have never known Paul to tell a lie. He is the best, kindest, most God-fearing man I have ever met! He would never lie! Not Paul!"

TEN

I opened the door and let Dehan into the room where Reverend Paul Truelove was sitting, staring at the pale gray tabletop in front of him that looked like the same color as his face. He looked up as we came in and watched us sit opposite him. Before I could speak, he said, "I was having an affair with Liz. If my parishioners had got to hear about it, or if the bishop had got to hear about it, particularly in view of her husband's condition, I would have been finished."

Dehan said, "So what happened?"

"I couldn't go to her. As you pointed out, it was a Sunday, the first Sunday in September, a fact that had completely escaped my mind after almost twenty years. I had a service and a sermon to deliver. So Elizabeth came to me. She slipped into the rectory while we were in worship, and once the service was finished, I joined her."

"Will she verify this?"

"Yes. She covered for me because I asked her to . . ."

I interrupted him. "You realize that if this is another lie . . ."

"I know! I know! You have made your point!" He was quiet for a moment. "I am not a liar, Detective Stone. I got trapped in a web of my own lies. The point is, I was lying to save my career, not to hide a murder!" We sat in silence for a moment. He looked from me to Dehan and back again. "Will the bishop have to hear about this?"

I suddenly felt tired and sick.

"I don't know yet. If it is not relevant to the murder, it is none of our business." I eyed him a moment and added, sourly, "But Reverend, in view of all this, don't you think you should be asking yourself if you're actually fit to be preaching sermons to people?"

He looked down at his hands. "Am I free to go?"

"Yeah. You are free to go."

He rose and left. The door closed behind him, and we sat for a bit without talking. Finally, I checked my watch and glanced at Dehan. "Let's grab a burger quick and then go see Frank."

"Did he call you?"

"No, but I'm sick of waiting."

As we walked down the stairs, I dialed his number. He answered after the first ring.

"Stone, I had my phone in my hand, I was just about to call you."

"Yeah, right. That is what you say to all the boys."

"It's actually on my desk. I'm reading it now. The pathologist was Mioko Itani. She isn't here anymore. She moved back to Japan. However, I should be able to answer most of your questions."

"Thanks, Frank."

We walked down to Banyer Place and bought two burgers, then walked slowly back up toward my car. Finally, she said, "I believe them."

I spoke around a mouthful of meat, salad, ketchup, and bun. "We can't afford to believe them, Dehan. We have to believe the evidence—which, I grant you, right now is telling us nothing. But if they are telling the truth, it means somebody else killed Simon

Martin." I wiped my mouth with the once white paper napkin and said, "So, if not them, then who . . . ?"

"I know. I know . . ."

I shrugged. "But I do agree with you, up to a point. We may have been on a wild goose chase. Maybe it is time we started looking a little farther afield . . ."

But even as I was saying it, I was only half believing myself. I climbed in behind the wheel and she got in beside me.

"When we get back," she said, "I will have a look, see if there were any other burglaries or house invasions in the area at the time."

I TOOK White Plains Road north, cruising at a nice, steady pace, watching the early onset of autumn: the first hint of russet in the plane trees against a pale blue sky, the first jackets and scarves replacing the T-shirts on the street, the lengthening shadows beginning to stretch out across the cooling sunlight on the sidewalks. I watched, and tried not to think. Sometimes, when you don't think, you see things clearer.

But Dehan had other ideas.

"Once, you told me I ought to think with my gut sometimes."

I glanced at her. "I must have been hungry."

"So here is what my gut is telling me right now. You want to hear?"

I nodded and kept watching the autumn.

"My gut tells me she was telling the truth about the insurance. You know why?"

"No."

"It was a rhetorical question, Stone. Just keep driving and let me talk."

"Okay."

"Because Sylvie Martin is the kind of woman who is always going to look for a domineering, controlling man to fix her problems. She married Simon and gravitated to Paul Truelove . . ."

I pulled the corners of my mouth down and danced my head around in a "you could be onto something" way.

"But!" She raised her index finger. "My gut also tells me that she remembers *exactly* what happened that night eighteen years ago."

I nodded in a more conventional fashion. "My gut agrees with your gut."

I turned onto Tremont, headed east.

"So," she said, "let's take baby steps. Let's state the obvious, one small step at a time: if she remembers what happened, that means she knows who the killer is."

"Almost certainly."

She turned in her seat to face me. "Okay, you're right. But then we have two options: either she knows, or she doesn't know because she didn't get a good look for one reason or another. Maybe he was wearing a balaclava, or it happened too fast and he had his back to her. But, if that is the case, then why the hell won't she talk? The only reason she would deliberately pretend to have amnesia is to conceal the identity of the killer."

I looked at her. "Yes, that is very solid reasoning."

She shrugged and spread her hands. "I can't think of another reason. Can you?"

"No. And I agree with you in your choice of words. You said 'conceal,' not 'protect.'" Then I sighed and shook my head. "But we are talking about intuition here, Dehan, which has practically no value. My gut tells me, as yours tells you, she is concealing the identity of the killer. It also tells me that she is not protecting him. How does that make sense? It doesn't. And unless we get some compelling evidence, all we have is verbose guts."

"Verbose guts?"

"You heard me right."

I turned into Silver Street and headed up Eastchester under the railway bridge and finally turned left at Morris Park and right onto Seminole Avenue. All the way we were silent. Maybe we were both listening to our verbose guts.

We found Frank in the small office annexed to his lab. He rose as we walked in.

"I don't know what you are hoping for, John. It is in the nature of these cold cases that the original investigating officer hadn't much to go on." He shrugged and smiled without much conviction. "That is why they went cold."

"I know. But sometimes things get overlooked. I am interested in the wound on his body."

"Why?"

I drew breath but Dehan smirked and said, "He's going to say, 'What is it about the wound that interests me?'" She grinned at me. "You were going to say that, weren't you?" She turned back to Frank. "He has this theory about how 'why' is a bad question. It works too. So here's the thing. There are two stab wounds right through the sternum. That in itself is odd, right? Who stabs through the sternum? So is there anything else you can tell us about the wounds that is interesting or unusual? Because the nature of the wounds is about all we have got right now to tell us anything about the killer."

We both stared at her. Frank blinked and said, "Okay. Come."

He picked up the Martin file and led us toward a projector on a bench. He switched it on and slid a photograph of Simon Martin's punctured chest into it. It magnified the image, and he pointed at the edges of the wound with the tip of his pen.

"I have read Mioko's notes and I agree with her conclusions. See how the lower edges of the puncture are smooth and taper into a kind of narrow *V* shape? Well, look now at the upper edge. There the skin is irregular and torn in a jagged pattern. Also note how the sides of the wound, about halfway up, are quite broad, giving it an elongated oval shape. All of this suggests that what we are looking at here is a broad-bladed bowie knife, serrated on the back side." He frowned at Dehan a moment. "You know the sort of thing, a survival knife, probably has a compass in the hilt."

"I know the sort of thing."

"Both stab wounds are very deep and quite close together, and both seem to kind of hook down, if you know what I mean. They enter the chest at the height of the second intercostals, and then penetrate downward at a slight angle into the heart."

I frowned, trying to visualize how the blow would be delivered. He saw my face and elaborated.

"It means one of two things, John. Either the blows were delivered overhand, in an arching motion, like so . . ." He demonstrated, holding his pen as though it were a lance, stabbing down at my chest. "Which presents certain problems. First of all, it is a very incompetent way to stab anybody, and practically nobody uses that method outside of black-and-white movies. But secondly, and more to the point, the angle it gives us is too acute. It penetrates the chest at a hundred and thirty-five degrees, and what we are looking for is more like a hundred degrees. Just past the dead-straight ninety-degree angle."

Dehan scratched her head. "So what is the other thing it might mean?"

He spread his hands. "Unless we say that it was delivered by a very tall man, lunging with the knife as though he were fencing . . ." He paused to demonstrate. ". . . in which case he would have to be a very strong, heavy man indeed to penetrate the sternum, I think our only other realistic scenario is that our victim is lying on his back, our killer straddles him, and using all the force of his weight, plunges the knife into his chest, in a kind of frenzy. Then we get the angle and the penetration that occured."

I scratched my chin. "A frenzy. But it's odd, isn't it? Hate frenzies usually result in ten, twenty, thirty, even more stab wounds. This is just two. Bam, bam, and we're done."

He nodded. "This is not that kind of frenzy. We had an abusive husband last month. He tormented his wife for years. Then one day, she snapped and stabbed him fifty times, over every inch of his body. No, this is not hatred. I would say this was more like fear. He was in a hurry to kill him and get out of there."

He switched the photograph and adjusted the focus and resolution. It showed the left side of Martin's rib cage. There was a large discoloration over his floating ribs. Then, he slid the lens up to his jaw, where there was another, and it had similar discoloration.

"These are the only bruises on his body. He has been hit twice in rapid succession with the right fist. He has fallen to the ground and immediately his assailant jumped on him, in a panic, plunged the knife twice into his chest, and fled."

Dehan asked the question that was on my mind. "Could a woman have done this?"

His face said he didn't like the idea. "A strong woman, using something other than her fist to strike the blows to his chest and jaw."

"So what you are suggesting here is a burglary gone wrong."

He wagged a finger at her. "I am suggesting nothing of the sort, young Dehan. It would certainly be consistent with a burglary gone wrong. But suggesting is for you and your partner, not me."

She looked at me, narrowing her eyes in frustration. "Why the hell would she want to conceal the identity of a burglar?" She held up her hands. "I know! Maybe it wasn't a burglar, maybe it was a lover. Maybe Simon walked in on her while she was shagging the reverend, but why the hell would she be shagging the reverend at the time she knew her husband was about to come home? And, who the hell takes a bowie knife along to a lovers' rendezvous?"

I nodded.

Frank shrugged. "Those are all good questions. What struck me as particularly interesting, though . . ." He rested his ass against the bench and wagged his pen at us. "Was both the similarities *and* the contrasts with the son's murder."

We stared at him, and he looked at us in turn. I said, "What?"

"The son. Jacob Martin. I assumed you knew. I thought you wanted me to look at both. You didn't know?"

Dehan was shaking her head. "She had a son? Who was stabbed to death? What the fuck?"

He frowned. "Sylvie Martin's son, Jacob. She was pregnant at the time her husband was killed. He was murdered fifteen years later, in surprisingly similar circumstances. Only the weapon was a little different. I assumed you knew."

ELEVEN

WE WENT BACK TO HIS OFFICE, AND AS I SAT HE HANDED me the file. Dehan sat next to me. Frank spoke as we leafed through the pages together.

"It was two years ago. Like the dad's murder, it was never solved. It must be filed in your own cold cases. What I can tell you is that he was found pretty much where his father was found, at the bottom of the stairs, lying on his back, and he had been stabbed in the heart, not twice, but six times. However, the stab wounds were *peri*mortem. There was very little bleeding. Other injuries, such as bruising and a broken neck, suggested that he might have fallen—or been pushed—down the stairs. The broken neck almost certainly killed him, and he was stabbed during death or immediately after."

"This," I said, tossing the file on the desk, "*was* a hate frenzy."

"Indeed."

Dehan put her fingertips to her forehead and closed her eyes, like she was trying really hard to understand something. "Why . . ." She held up her hands to me. "Sorry, *what* would make Sylvie Martin not tell us about her son? And what the hell would make the reverend not mention it either? This is a conspiracy of silence. There is no two ways about it."

I nodded. "I agree. It just isn't conceivable. You do not simply omit to mention something like this." I frowned. "Why the hell wasn't it flagged and cross-referenced?"

Frank shrugged. "For us it was. But you're talking about an eighteen-year-old cold case, and from the Bronx, what's more. Computerizing and cross-referencing requires money and manpower, two commodities I'm guessing the Forty-Third is short on."

I made to stand. "You got that right, Frank." I paused. "The weapon the boy was killed with . . ."

"My best guess, a large kitchen knife. One down from the cleaver with a very solid blade, and very, very sharp."

BACK AT THE STATION, I dug out the Jacob Martin file and set about studying it, while Dehan started plowing through burglaries in the East Bronx area during the last six months of 1999, a task which gave a whole new meaning to the phrase, "can't see the wood for the trees."

Jacob had been almost fifteen and a half when he was killed. He'd been found by his mother, lying at the bottom of the stairs, in a similar position to that of her husband. Where her husband had been stabbed twice, Jacob's chest was riddled with deep stab wounds. He'd had several fractured ribs, a broken wrist, multiple bruises, and a broken neck. The number of injuries, and the degree of severity, were consistent with having been propelled down the stairs with some serious force.

The murder weapon was not found, despite a search of the house, the garden, and the gardens and trash cans of the neighborhood. There was no knife missing from the Martins' block, and lab analysis of the knives in the block revealed no blood residue—other than pork and beef.

As before, the locks had not been forced. Sylvie and Mary had been at a church fête at the time, and Sylvie had found Jacob's body on returning home. The date of the murder had been the fifth of September, 2015.

It could not be a coincidence.

I threw the file on the desk and went to get coffee. I felt unreasonably angry. Halfway there, I turned back and walked up to Dehan, who was engrossed in her laptop and making notes on a pad.

"You want coffee?"

"Thanks."

I stalked back to the machine and got two cups of the oh-so-lovely black liquid. I carried them back and put one next to her.

"You're not going to find anything. It's a pointless exercise. There is no way these two murders are a coincidence."

"Mm-hm."

"You know what date he was killed?"

She glanced at me, said nothing, and carried on making notes.

"Fifth of September."

"Huh!"

I sighed and rubbed my face. I looked at her and noticed she had tied her hair in a knot behind her head, then wondered why I would notice that. It made her neck look nice. I sighed.

"You seeing your uncle again tonight?"

She narrowed her eyes at me and carried on making notes.

I persisted, trying to talk the irritation I was feeling out of my system. "You want to come over? We'll throw some steaks on the barbeque and see if we can work this damn thing out."

"I can't."

I nodded. "Oh. What's stopping you?"

"My uncle. He wants me to go over and visit."

"Cool. Good. Enjoy. How you getting on?"

She ignored me for three or four minutes, then flopped back in her chair and picked up her notebook.

"Okay, this was like looking for a very particular piece of hay in a haystack. But I managed to sift and filter out the irrelevant and came up with this, which might be significant."

"Hit me with it."

"Mention my uncle again and I might." She glared at me for a second and continued. "Okay, so in the period January to December, 1999, we have a spate of burglaries in the area between Bronxdale Avenue in the west, Lurting Avenue in the east, Van Nest in the north, and Sacket in the south . . ."

"East Bronx."

"Pretty much."

I shrugged. "But we get that every year. It's called living in the Bronx."

"Shut up, don't be a smart-ass right now."

"Okay."

"The particular burglaries I am talking about were all confessed to by one guy. His thefts were always pretty neat. He was a locksmith. He would pick the locks, leaving practically no trace. He would choose times when there is nobody at home and leave no trace of his having been there, except a couple of times he left the back door open, probably because he left in a hurry and didn't want to make a noise." She raised a finger to stop me talking. "Now, interesting point is, there are no reported cases of violence in any of these burglaries. *Except,* he was caught because in the last case, the house owner came home early. Our guy attacked him with a knife, but the owner was a huge guy and a martial arts instructor, so he absolutely decked him. Our boy is Julio Beltran, El Chato, who, though never convicted, is suspected of several crimes involving violence and knife attacks. He is a known member of the Sureños."

She dropped the pad on the desk and studied my face. I shook my head. "What would make Sylvie Martin lie to conceal El Chato's identity? It doesn't make any sense. Where is he now?"

"He did time. Now he seems to be going straight. Runs his own business, Key Solutions, a locksmith shop, surprisingly enough."

"Was he out two years ago?"

She nodded. "Yup."

I scowled and said, "Great!"

She made a face of reluctance. "I'm sorry."

I laughed without mirth. "It's not your fault."

"No. I mean I'm sorry I can't come over for the barbeque."

I waved a hand at her. "Ah, no sweat. I'm glad you're having fun."

She sighed noisily through her nose. It may have been a suppressed snarl. "You want to go see him?"

I stood. "Why not?"

EL CHATO HAD his premises on the corner of Rhineland Avenue and White Plains Road. It was a narrow, three-story building painted an obnoxious bright yellow, with the living accommodation upstairs and the shop on the ground floor.

The front door was mainly glass and plywood, with flaking, desiccated varnish peeling off like dandruff on a balding scalp. As I pushed it open, an electronic notifier mocked us with an *ee-oh* sound, then another as it closed. Behind the counter, a big Mexican in his mid to late thirties stood up from a workbench to look at us. I glanced around. He sold belts and boot polish, fixed shoes and handbags, and also made keys. You could tell by his expression that he knew who we were. He leaned his elbows on the counter and said, "I know you don't just want duplicates for your keys."

We showed him our badges. "I'm Detective Stone, this is Detective Dehan. Are you Julio Beltran?"

"Yup." He had the expression of a man who has stopped wincing because he knows the blow is coming anyway. "What can I do for you, Detectives?"

"We're just looking for some information. Back in 1999, you did a series of jobs in East Bronx."

He nodded. "For which I served my time, attended my courses, and have stayed out of trouble ever since."

Dehan said, "We are not questioning that, Julio. But 'round that time, in September, there was a break-in on Bogart Avenue. You know anything about that?"

He pulled a face and shook his head. "Nothin' to do with me." He straightened up. "When they caught me, that guy almost killed me. He broke my jaw, four ribs, an' my right elbow." He pointed at Dehan. "Best thing that ever happen to me. That guy's name is Gunnar Olafsen. An' he is now my best friend, and my sensei. You know that?"

I sighed. "That is very touching."

"No, I'm serious, man. He scared the shit out of me. I thought I was gonna die that night, but he knew when to stop. See what I mean? That's what I learnt. Know when to stop. Then he called the ambulance an' the cops. An' after that he used to come and visit me in the jail. He talked to me. He convinced me to make a new start. I owe that guy my life. Two times over at that. So what I'm tellin' you. I came clean. I told the cops everythin'. Clean slate."

Dehan raised an eyebrow at him. "What about the knife fights and the woundings?"

He made an ugly face that said she was stupid and waved a hand at her. "*Anda por ahí ya, pendeja!* That was nothin' to do with you! That was between us. None of the cops' fockin' business. We have our disagreements and we solve them ourselves." He shook a finger at her. "But it was *within* the Sureños, eh? It did not involve anybody outside. It was private matters of ours. None of your goddamn business."

I said, "Do you know Sylvie Martin?"

He shrugged and spread his hands. "No . . ."

"You ever been involved with the St. George's Methodist Church on Fowler Avenue?"

He stared at me. "Oh, now wait a minute. Bogart Avenue? That the one that's parallel to Fowler?"

I frowned, nodded.

He sighed and spread his arms wide, like he was a victim on the cross. "C'mon, man!" He kind of staggered away, then came back, looking at us like we were being unreasonable. "You gotta be kidding me. The house that backs onto the church? The cute blonde?"

We didn't say anything. We just watched him and waited for it. He shook his finger in the negative. "You ain't gonna pin nothing on me there. I never broke into that house. I was gonna. It was on my list. Okay? I am coming clean with you. I was gonna break in. But man, she was always in the goddamn house! An' if she wasn't there, that fockin' kid, the gardener, was there. An' the one time I got into the back garden, that fockin' freak from the church was hiding in the bushes, sees me, an' starts screaming and hitting me! Like the fockin' hunchback of Notre-fockin-Dame!" He surprised me and burst out laughing. "*El Diavolo! El Diavolo!*"

I held up a hand. "Let me get this straight, Julio. You staked out the house . . ."

He nodded. "Yeah. It was one of the houses I had on my list. I was an apprentice locksmith. We did some work at the house. Upgraded the locks or something, I don't recall. Anyways, it was on my list. I staked it out a couple of nights. But it wasn't worth the fockin' risk, man. She was always either at home or in the church. The Arab kid was always in the garden. Then that weird fockin' freak scared the shit out of me and I moved on. I guess God was givin' me a warning. I should'a paid heed, huh?"

Dehan and I stared at each other for a moment. Then I looked at El Chato. "Who was your boss?"

He grabbed one of his business cards and scribbled on the back. "Klive's Keys. He won't give me a good reference, you know what I mean? But he'll confirm I was working for him."

"Okay." I took the card. "Where were you two years ago?"

He shrugged. "Here. Where else?"

I nodded and we turned to go. At the door, he called me back. "Hey, Detective. What was it, a homicide?"

I nodded. "Yeah. Why?"

He kind of winced. "Was it her? She had a baby girl . . ."

I shook my head. "No."

"Oh, okay."

We left.

TWELVE

I LEANED MY HEAD ON THE CAR AND SHE STOOD staring down the long, ugly road in the late-afternoon sun, like she was looking at the view. After a bit, she said, "Okay, I am willing to bet that there is a fifty-fifty chance that if we search El Chato's house, we will find a bowie knife, or something similar. But what we are not going to find are any Oscars, or even any awards for junior drama. I grew up with these guys, Stone, and he is exactly what he seems to be. He has an IQ between ninety-eight and one hundred and two. He is bog-standard average. There is no way this guy is going to make up that story, thinking on his feet."

I shrugged one shoulder. "Maybe."

"Let me tell you the problem I'm having. I can think of one person, and only one person, who fits the bill. He's big enough to knock Simon down, strong enough to stab him through the sternum, close enough to Sylvie to be in her house, obsessed enough with her to go violently to her aid if he thought she needed protecting, and simple enough not to realize that stabbing her husband in the heart was way out of proportion to the telling off he was giving his wife."

"I know."

"And, maybe most important of all, it might explain why she is concealing his identity."

I looked down at my shoes. "We agree that Humberto is possibly Paul's son."

"I would lay money on it."

"We need to confirm it."

"I am thinking Humberto makes a habit of slinking around hiding in the bushes and peering through Sylvie's window. He has got a childish crush on her, which to *him* it is like she is the center of the universe. And we know that there is easy access from the church to the house via the back gardens.

"I am thinking, on that Sunday, Ahmed finishes his work and Humberto sees him leave. He sneaks into the garden and finds the back door open. He goes in. Just then, Simon arrives."

She paused, thinking.

I said, "We know that she hadn't put the lights on and she wasn't at the door to greet him."

Dehan nodded. "Maybe that made Simon the Patriarch mad. Maybe he was having a go at her, threatening fire and brimstone for being a Jezebel, or whatever. Who knows? Thing is, Humberto comes to her aid."

"Meanwhile, Paul is making hay with Elizabeth. But after the cops have gone, he phones and they talk for almost an hour. She is shaken, but not totally unhappy with the result. She is now financially secure, and free of her husband. They agree to keep Humberto's name out of it." I chewed my lip for a bit. "But where the hell did Humberto get a bowie knife?"

Dehan stared at me a moment. "Wasn't Daddy an intrepid explorer on the Amazon?"

I stood and opened the car. "We need to confirm that. We need to know what their relationship is." I hesitated and looked at my watch. "You need to be somewhere . . ."

She looked uncomfortable, stood on her toes, and shook her head. "Yeah . . . no, I can get a cab. Where are you going?"

"I'm going to go and scare the bejaysus out of Elizabeth."

She nodded. "That makes sense. Find out what really happened in Brazil."

"I can drop you somewhere."

"Nah, it's not on your way."

"Where is he picking you up, at the precinct?"

"Uh-huh."

"Come on, I will drop you there."

She sighed and climbed in. As she slammed the door, she said, "I really should bring my own car."

I fired up the engine. "For tomorrow, you can bring your own car. Today I can give you a lift."

". . . I didn't mean that."

We didn't talk again till we got to the 43rd. I pulled up at the corner and looked through the window. Outside, the afternoon was turning to dusk. There was a convertible Mercedes sports car parked in the lot. A good-looking guy in his early thirties was sitting against the trunk. Dehan sat staring at the dash.

"We are here."

"I know. Will you pick me up tomorrow?"

"Sure, if you want me to."

She looked at me with intense, black eyes. "Yes, please."

She got out and I watched her walk toward the guy with the sick car. He smiled at her and stood, bent to kiss her. She gave him her cheek and they climbed in the car. I pulled away and headed for Eastchester Bay.

By the time I got to Elizabeth Cavendish's house it was getting dark. The streetlamps were glowing amber, and the cars were made invisible by the glare of their dull headlamps. I pulled into her drive and rang the bell. After a moment, she opened the door and stood looking at me. I could smell the gin on her breath, and she was a little unsteady on her feet. I could hear the music and sporadic chatter of a movie coming from her living room.

"This I didn't expect. Where is your cute partner? Is this a social call?"

"No, Mrs. Cavendish. I have some questions for you. I would really appreciate five minutes of your time."

She gave a nicotine-stained grunt. "How disappointing." Then she turned and walked away. I took that as an invitation and stepped inside, closing the door behind me.

In the living room, she picked up the remote and turned off the TV.

"Will you have a drink?"

"No, thank you."

"Less and less fun."

She dropped onto her sofa and pointed to a chair. I sat.

"Mrs. Cavendish, do you understand that if you cover for somebody who is guilty of murder, you are committing a very serious crime?"

She went very serious but did not answer.

I pressed on. "More to the point, if you enabled that person to commit the crime, whether you knew there would be a murder or not, you would be equally as guilty as they are. Do you fully appreciate what is involved in helping somebody to commit, or cover up, a homicide?"

"I think I want you to leave now."

I shook my head. "No, you don't. Because if I leave now, you leave with me, in cuffs."

She went pale. "What is this, some sick, sexual game? Is this how you get your kicks?"

I watched her a moment. "I want you to be fully aware of the risks you are taking on Paul's behalf. I know he wasn't here on the night of Simon's death. I know you were there. I know he phoned Sylvie from the rectory and I know they talked for almost an hour. And I know that *you* know a damn sight more than you are telling me." I pointed at her. "But you need to understand that you could wind up doing serious time. And believe me, for a woman like you, a state pen is not a good place to be."

She was rigid and her hand had started trembling. "You're threatening me."

"Threatening? No, warning." I shrugged. "Semantics. You need to think long and hard about how you answer my next questions. Think," I said, "about who is going to look after Reggie while you are on the inside for trying to protect Paul."

"What do you want to know?"

"Who is Humberto?"

She seemed to sag and covered her face with her left hand. "No . . ."

"I'm serious, Elizabeth. Is he Paul's son?"

She nodded into her hand. "Of course he is."

"Why all the cloak-and-dagger? Why all the secrecy? Paul is an American citizen. Why didn't he just register him as his son?"

She heaved a sigh and dropped her hand. "Because, in the first place, he was conceived out of wedlock. In the second place, the girl who conceived him was, putting it bluntly, of mixed race *and* she was a whore. To enlightened people like you and me, that may mean nothing, but to the people who make up Reverend Paul Truelove's congregation, both of those facts carry a lot of weight. If they had found out that he'd been making the beast with two backs with a blackberry tart, they would have dumped him before he could bellow, 'I'm coming!'"

She reached for a packet of cigarettes and lit one with shaking hands. She inhaled deeply, stood, and carried her drink out to the patio, where she stood leaning against the wall, staring at her pool. I followed and stood in the doorway behind her. The turquoise water looked luminous and translucent. The croaking of the frogs was loud.

"Okay, I understand his decision to keep his paternity a secret from his congregation. But, if he went to the trouble of bringing him into the country, why didn't he register his birth, or adopt him? The kid is a ghost. He has no Social Security number, no birth certificate . . ."

She interrupted me, half shouting, "Because he's wanted for murder in Brazil!"

"*What?* He hasn't the mental capacity for murder . . ."

She turned to glare at me. "Do you think they give a damn about that? He killed the son of the local *cacique*. It was an accident, but that makes fuck all difference to them! They mean to get hold of him, by fair means or foul, and Paul, for once in his miserable life, is doing the right thing." She moved to the table and sat. A spasm of irritation contracted her face. "Oh, for God's sake, get yourself a drink and stop being so damned upright!"

I went to the trolley and poured myself a couple of inches of Irish. She waited for me to sit before she started talking again. Then, to the lapping of the pool and the sawing of the frogs, she told me the story of Humberto and Paul.

THIRTEEN

"Paul was supposed to be doing missionary work for the church. Of course, he saw that as an opportunity to make large sums of money under the table, by cultivating influential friends and getting involved in various forms of contraband and smuggling. Only God knows what he got up to. Or perhaps He doesn't. Knowing Him, He is probably turning a blind eye." She stared a moment at the light, warping liquid silver on the surface of the pool under a black sky. There was something tragic in her once beautiful face. "That man had truly no conscience and no inhibitions. We were in the Andirá-Marau region, in Itaituba, on the river Tapajós. It is a tributary of the Amazon, a hellhole miles from anywhere. It was remote. And I do mean, *remote.*"

"What were you doing there?"

"Reggie worked for a pharmaceutical company. He was engaged in research of the rainforest. We met Paul at a dinner party. He and Reggie hit it off, and I confess I found him fascinating. You would not think so to meet him now, but when he's not putting on his pompous Man-of-God act, he is a very exciting, totally immoral bastard. Sorry."

"So what happened?"

She didn't answer for a moment. She sucked on her cigarette

like she was hungry for the smoke. The only sound was the slap of the water and the sawing of the frogs down by the river.

"He had befriended one of the local land barons, Gabriel da Silva. They were involved in some shady deals together, something to do with logging." She held a hand up to me. "Don't ask me. I stayed out of that kind of thing. I was not and am not interested. The point is, Paul had rented this big, colonial villa on the lake just outside town. He had invited da Silva, his wife, and son to dinner. The boy was about thirteen—a little streak of piss of a kid. They all had a pretty unenlightened attitude toward the staff, as you can imagine. Human life hasn't much value in those parts of the world."

She stopped talking. I sipped my whiskey and reached for her cigarettes. She watched me light up and smiled a triumphant smile.

"Careful, big boy. Don't lose control completely. You never know where you'll end up sleeping tonight."

I raised an eyebrow at her and allowed myself a smile. "Don't stop, keep going."

She sighed. "Reggie and I were invited. And of course Luz, his whore, and their son, Humberto. You know? I really believe Luz was the only woman he ever truly loved." She shrugged. "She was bad and cheap and fake . . . like him, I guess. She meant something to him. Humberto was about twelve, I suppose. But even then he was a damned freak, almost six feet and terrifyingly strong."

She paused, picking a piece of tobacco from her lip with her index finger. She examined it a moment and carried on talking.

"Humberto has this thing, where he becomes obsessively attached to women. Probably because his mother was an ice queen who was always fobbing him off onto their black nanny, Carmela. He adored Carmela. Anyway, I don't know exactly what happened, but on this particular night, before dinner, Humberto and this boy Gonzalo were in the pool. Gonzalo was tormenting Humberto mercilessly, as he always did. He enjoyed it because

Humberto was so much bigger and stronger, but with the mind of a child, it was so easy to terrorize him."

She sighed, stubbed out her cigarette, and reached for another. I lit it for her. She drew in the smoke and let it out in puffs as she spoke.

"Naturally, Paul and Luz were not going to intervene, and Gabriel and his wife, whatever her name was, thought it was all terribly amusing. Reggie only cared about his cut of whatever deal was going down and I, well, I'm sorry, but however distasteful I may have found it, I wasn't going to get involved. So that just left Carmela, the black nanny. Frankly, she handled it very well. She came out with a towel and told Humberto it was time to get out of the pool and come in for his supper. I think Paul was relieved. I know I was, and I am damned certain Humberto was. He clung to her like she was his guardian angel. Poor freak was sobbing his eyes out."

"So what happened?"

"What happened was that little Gonzalo got mad at having his fun spoiled. He got out of the pool, on his skinny little legs, and started screaming at Carmela that she was a *'puta negra,'* a black whore, and how dare she break up their fun. I remember it so clearly . . ."

She turned to look at me. The amber light from the spots lay across the drawn planes of her face, casting her eyes into shadow.

"Humberto protected her?"

"It was worse than that. I can see him now, the nasty little runt, his skin all wet and glistening in the lights from the house, and the spotlights from the pool. He was like a dancing, wriggling worm, stamping his feet and shouting. It should have been comical, but he started slapping Carmela, screaming at her. It happened in a matter of seconds. I can see it so vividly: Gabriel and his wife half standing, laughing, calling to Gonzalo to stop, Paul getting to his feet, looking embarrassed, poor Carmela cowering away . . ."

I felt the heat from the cigarette on my fingers and stubbed it out. Her gaze was lost in her glass. The drink was gone and the ice had melted. I said, "And Humberto?"

She gave a little shake of her head, like she was taken aback about what she was about to say.

"He punched him, like a boxer. Two great thumps with his right fist. Gonzalo fell, and Humberto sat on him and started pounding him again and again. Everybody ran, screaming. Carmela was trying to drag him off, so was Paul. Gabriel and his wife were trying to drag Gonzalo from under him. It seemed to go on for an eternity. I saw his huge, balled fist hit Gonzalo's head three or four times, maybe more. He was bleeding badly. His eyes were kind of goggling and out of focus. He wasn't even trying to defend himself. It was horrible."

"He was dead?"

She handed me her glass. "Get me another drink, would you?"

I stood and moved to the trolley. I started putting together a gin and tonic. Her voice followed me.

"You know? I have never talked about this. It's kind of therapeutic. I suppose if I had been sensible, I would have gotten myself a therapist. But I don't go in for that kind of stuff. Stiff upper lip, and a stiff drink to go with it." I heard the smile in her voice. "I'm watching you. Don't drown the gin."

I gave her the drink and smiled. "Just don't get drunk before you've told me the story."

"After that, have I got permission?"

"After that, you can drink yourself into oblivion, if you so wish."

"I do wish," she said sourly, and drank. "They tried to revive him, there by the pool. Paul wanted to call an ambulance, but Gabriel stopped him. He said it would take too long, they would take him in the car." She shook her head. "I could see he was already gone. His skin was pasty and gray. His eyes were open, and he wasn't breathing. His mother was hysterical, screaming that he was dead." She mimicked her without compassion, "'*Está morto! Está morto!*' They rushed him out to the car and bundled him in the back. And just before they left, Gabriel went up to Paul, and I have never seen anything so horrific and evil and terrifying in my life. He put his face right up close and spat at him. He said that if Gonzalo was dead, Humberto would die too, and Paul would spend the rest of his life in Monte Cristo, a notorious prison in Amazonia, where he would be tortured until he begged for death."

"What did you do?"

"Paul made an executive decision, as he needed to. He was probably right in this case. He said if we stuck around and waited for the police, or if we handed ourselves in, we were as good as dead. Especially him, Humberto, and Carmela. He said we had to go, right then and there. He had a boat moored by the house and we should use that to get to Macapá, where we could get passage to the U.S.A. The moron of his whore insisted on collecting her jewels and her clothes. That delayed us, and it cost her her life, and almost cost Reggie his."

"Gabriel came back?"

She nodded. "Yes, he came back, with his farmhands. They got Luz in the house. I don't want to even imagine what they did to the stupid bitch. Reggie was shot in the head just as he was clambering aboard the boat." She paused, looking into her drink. "They didn't kill him, but it might have been better if they had." She sighed and shrugged. "God alone knows how we didn't kill ourselves that night. We must have been doing forty miles an hour down the river, dodging logs and heaven knows what else. We dropped Carmela at Fordlândia . . ."

"Where?"

"Don't laugh. It is actually called that. Fordlândia. She had family there. We eventually made it to Santarém, where Paul bought another boat and we got medical attention for Reggie. It cost a small fortune in bribes to buy the doctors' silence, but we managed it. Then we sailed on to Macapá, where we bought papers for Humberto and caught a ship for New York. If you have money in Brazil, you can buy anything. And anyone."

I drained my glass. "I am going to need names, dates . . . the name of the ship . . . I'll need you to make a formal statement."

"I know."

"I won't use the information if I don't have to. But you understand that Humberto may have killed again, twice."

She nodded. "God, what a mess."

"That night, the night of Simon's murder, where was Humberto?"

She shook her head. "I assumed he was with Paul at the church."

"Did Paul say anything to you, after he phoned Sylvie?"

"No. Just that there had been a break-in and that Simon had been killed."

I stood. She watched me. Her expression was both strong and pathetic. She smiled. It wasn't a happy smile. "I don't suppose you want to stay?"

I smiled back. It was the same kind of smile. "Thanks. I'm spoken for."

"How delightfully old-fashioned of you."

I left her at the door, climbed into my ancient Jaguar, and headed home, thinking about my choice of words. Spoken for. An ancient Latin phrase crept into my head. *Res ipsa loquitor*: the thing speaks for itself.

That was me. The thing. The dinosaur speaks for itself.

FOURTEEN

THE NEXT MORNING IT WAS DRIZZLING FROM A LOW ceiling of heavy cloud. Dehan was waiting in the doorway of her apartment block and dodged across the road when she saw me coming. She climbed in and slammed the door as I pulled back into the traffic. I tried out a smile.

"How was your evening?"

She shrugged. "How did it go with Elizabeth Cavendish?"

"It is quite a story."

She listened in silence as I recounted it. When I had finished, she said, "So what are you thinking? It kind of supports what we were saying yesterday."

"On the face of it." I threw her a smile. "Prima facie." She didn't respond. I went on. "So I am thinking I need to break Paul down and get the truth out of him. At the same time, I think I would like a warrant to search the church, the rectory, and the grounds."

"What about Sylvie?"

I shook my head. "Right now, trying to talk to Sylvie is a waste of time. She'll just keep seeking refuge in her supposed amnesia. I think she has almost come to believe it herself. No, we need to appeal to Paul's self-interest. Not Reverend Truelove, but the real Paul, the amoral Amazonian adventurer."

She cocked her head to one side. "He sounds like a man who'd go a long way to protect his son."

"Up to a point, you're right. But he has a pretty warped sense of what protection means, hasn't he? He did risk his own life to get him out of Brazil, but he wouldn't risk his business deal to protect his son from a bully."

She turned away and gazed out the window at the wet people hunched under their umbrellas, jostling each other on the passing sidewalk.

"True."

After a bit, I asked her, "You all right?"

She looked surprised but didn't smile. "Sure. Why wouldn't I be?"

"I don't know. You seem distracted."

"I'm fine."

WE CLIMBED the stairs to the captain's office in silence and I tapped on the door.

"Come!"

I opened the door for Dehan and she stared at me blankly, so I went in ahead of her. The captain beamed when he saw us and stood, reaching for our hands like we were the guests of honor at his restaurant.

"Stone! Dehan! Come in, come in, sit. I have been expecting you to show up." He laughed. "You were about due!"

He sat as we sat, smiling. The corners of his eyes creased around his graying temples, making him look comfortable and reassuring.

"To turn JFK on his head, let me ask you, what can your police department do for you?"

He expected a laugh, so I gave him one. Then, I explained the case in some detail, told him there was a sergeant at Elizabeth Cavendish's house right then taking her statement, explained about Humberto's ambiguous legal status, and told him I wanted to interview him in the presence of his putative father, while at the same time conducting a search of the church, the rectory, and the grounds.

When I had finished, he flopped back in his chair. "You sure know how to pick 'em, I'll give you that. See if you can get the reverend's permission for the search, will you? It'll be interesting to know how he reacts. If he says no, we will apply for a court order. I'll contact social services and discuss the status of the boy. You think he did it?"

I shook my head. "It is very hard to tell at this stage, sir. At the very least we need to eliminate him as a suspect. There are other possibilities . . ."

He nodded. "The reverend and Sylvie themselves, I should have thought, jointly or severally. Julio Beltran; his story may be very credible, but it may just be no more than that!" He grinned. "We Latinos are a very creative people, you know, John! Am I right, Carmen?"

The smile she gave him had a miraculous quality to it, like water coming out of a stone.

I nodded. "I am sure, sir, and it is early days. There may still be angles we have not yet uncovered. This case has a way of throwing up surprises."

He laid both hands palm down on the desk. "Good! Exceptional work as always, both of you. Choose your team for the search. Carry on!"

As we were going down the stairs, I phoned Reverend Truelove.

"Good morning, Detective. I have been expecting your call."

"I figured. Elizabeth called you last night, I guess."

"Yes. I suppose you want me to come in."

"Not exactly." I entered the detectives' room and rested my ass on the edge of my desk. Dehan dropped into her chair. "I would like you to bring Humberto in to talk to me. I would like you to sit in on the interview. Bring a lawyer if you think you'll need one."

"I see . . ."

"Don't be a runner on me, Paul. This is not Brazil, and we are not gunning for him. Whether he did it or not, he needs help, and you need to get his situation straightened out. He is a vulnerable person and he needs protecting."

"Yes. I understand that, and you are right."

"I want something else too, and I am hoping you are going to cooperate with me."

"What is that?"

"I want to search the church, everything."

"What do you think you're going to find?"

I hesitated. "The murder weapon."

He grunted. "Hmmm, I have often wondered about that. There is not much point in my saying no, is there? If I do, you will get a search warrant and the proverbial shit will hit the fan. Besides, I would like you to see I actually have nothing to hide. Yes, go ahead. We'll be there in twenty minutes."

I hung up. Dehan was watching me. I said, "You want to pick a team and search the church? Go over everything with a fine-tooth comb. Use your judgment. We are looking for a bowie knife and a large kitchen knife. Maybe they threw them in the trash, maybe they threw them in the river. Maybe they never had them in the first place. Maybe we will get lucky and they are buried in the garden."

She stood. "Got it. I'll get an unmarked . . ."

I reached in my pocket, pulled out my keys, and threw them to her. "Take mine."

She frowned. "You sure?"

"You've driven it halfway across the country, I think you'll be all right driving it as far as the East Bronx."

". . . Thanks."

. . .

Twenty minutes later, Maria called me from the desk to say that Reverend Truelove and Humberto had arrived. I went to fetch them and led them up to interview room three. Humberto was smiling a lot, like he thought the whole thing was a great gas. That didn't surprise me so much. But the reverend was looking more resigned than worried, and that did. I wondered if it was because he thought the spotlight was off him and onto his son.

They sat side by side and I smiled at Humberto. He grinned back at me and made that sound teenage boys make when they're embarrassed and they laugh, like a braying donkey.

I addressed his father. "Reverend, am I right in thinking that Humberto understands us when we speak English?"

"Up to a point, yes. But his vocabulary is limited." He spread his hands. "It is limited by his mental capacity."

I turned to his son. "Humberto, *eu sou John. Tu es Humberto.*"

He laughed like a kid who just got his favorite toy for Christmas.

I put my hand on my chest, then reached across and put my hand on his chest. "*Eu e voce, amigos.*"

It was like I had busted a dam. His voice was huge as he bellowed with a total lack of inhibition.

"*Deo gratia! E un angelo! E un angelo! Voce angelo. Gratia Maria! Misericordia! Gratia!*" And he laughed, rubbing his vast hands all over his face and his head, leaning against his father. "*Amigo! Amigo!*"

The reverend said, "You probably gather. He says you are an angel, and he is thanking Mary for your friendship."

"Doesn't he think of Sylvie as Mary?"

"Any woman whom he favors can become the Sacred Mother."

"*Mater Sancta, Maria . . .*"

I put my hand on my chest again. "*Eu, voce, Maria Sylvie, amigos.*"

He was still smiling, but now his eyes were studying me. He spoke more quietly. "*Angelo, angelo di la guarda. Humberto, angelo di la guarda, santisima madre, fili et pater noster, angelo di la guarda.*"

I looked at Paul. "Is he saying that he is Sylvie's guardian angel?"

"In as much as he is speaking coherently at all, Detective, he is identifying himself as her guardian angel, yes. I think she once jestingly called him that and he liked it."

I gave Humberto the thumbs-up and pushed a little further. "*Eu, voce, Maria Sylvie, e Simon . . .*"

He groaned loudly, dropped his head on the table, and covered it with his arms. "*None! None! Diavolo incarnato, note oscura, santaficata Maria! Santaficata Maria! None! None!*"

"Is he calling Simon the devil incarnate?"

He sighed. "I don't know what you hope to achieve with this, Detective."

I leaned closer toward Humberto. "*Diavolo incarnato?*"

Paul interrupted, "*Onde voce ollo a diavolo incarnato?*"

"*No jardim de Getsêmani! Santa Maria plena di graza! Fora! Fora! Fora!*"

He started covering his head again. Paul placed his hand gently on his shoulder. "I asked him where he had seen the devil incarnate. He said he had seen him in the Garden of Gethsemane."

"What does that mean?"

"It could be simple fantasy . . ."

"Does he hallucinate?"

He was taken aback. "Well, no, I have never known him to . . ."

"Then why would this be fantasy?"

"I simply mean . . ."

"I am getting tired of you putting obstacles in my way at every step of this investigation, Paul. You are not doing yourself any favors. At the moment, I am trying harder than you know to help you and Humberto. Keep trying to sabotage me and you will lose my support. Have I made myself understood? You are running out of credit."

He drew breath. "He may have seen somebody in Sylvie's garden. He has referred to her garden as Gethsemane in the past."

"He did. I know he did. He scared off a burglar shortly before Simon was killed." He looked astonished, but I ignored him and turned back to Humberto. I put my hand on his huge arm. "*Angelo de la guarda. Voce, e eu. Maria Sylvie e Simon.*"

He kept his head covered, muttering, "*Malo, malefico, diavolo incarnato, muita sanguis nas manos, muita sanguis no punhal, muita sanguis, malo malefica, diavolo incarnato, Santa Maria . . . Santa Maria . . .*"

He went quiet, but for the sound of his sobs. I looked at Paul.

He sighed again. "He keeps saying it is bad, the devil incarnate had blood on his hands, lots of blood on the dagger. But this does not constitute a confession of any sort, Detective. He could be talking about a film he has seen. It could be anything."

"You and I both know exactly what it means, Reverend. What did you talk to Sylvie about for forty-five minutes on the phone the night Simon was killed?"

"I called when I saw the police had left to see if she was all right."

"Why didn't you go over?"

"She told me not to."

"Did she tell you Humberto had been there?"

"No!"

Humberto looked up. His face was wet. "*Amigo. Angelo di la guarda.*"

"Did she tell you who had killed Simon?"

"No. She said she wanted to forget."

"Was it Humberto?"

"No . . . !" He hesitated. "I don't know."

I turned to Humberto. "Did Simon hurt Sylvie, Humberto?"

"*Malo, diavolo . . .*"

"Did you stop him from hurting Sylvie? Did you stop Simon from hurting Sylvie?"

He grinned. "Humberto, *angelo di la guarda, Santa Maria plena di graza . . .*"

My phone rang. I looked at the screen. It was Dehan. I glanced at Paul. "Excuse me." I stepped out of the room into the corridor and answered.

"Yeah."

"Stone. I think you're going to want to come and see this. We found both knives. It's like a hoard, or a stash of treasures. It's in the grounds, in the hedgerow by the fence. The bowie knife is in a plastic bag. The kitchen knife isn't. I think there's still blood caked on both weapons."

I was quiet for a moment. "Okay, I'll be there in twenty minutes. Have you called the CSI team?"

"Yeah. They are already on their way."

"Don't let them take anything away till I get there. Here is what I want you to do . . ."

I stepped back into the room and sat. I smiled at Humberto. He grinned. I put a sentence together I hoped he would understand. "*Eu quiero ollare votre tesoro.*"

He laughed his donkey bray laugh. "*Voce, eu, ollare meu tesoro!*"

Paul frowned. "He is going to show you his treasure? What treasure?"

"Let's find out."

FIFTEEN

I STEPPED OUT OF THE REVEREND'S CAR ONTO THE WET
sidewalk, in the damp, gray afternoon. Paul got out of the driver's
side and helped Humberto out of the back, then led him around
to where I was waiting. We walked together through the gate and
into the grounds of the church. Outside the big, red doors, a
uniformed cop watched us. I stopped and said to Paul, "Don't say
anything." Then I smiled at Humberto and repeated, "I want to
see your treasure. *Eu quiero ollare votre tesoro.*"

He gripped my arm in a powerful hand, grinning widely, and
led me at a shambling run along the path toward the garden where
the fête had been held just a few days earlier. I saw Dehan and half
a dozen cops standing back, as I had asked her to on the phone.
They watched Humberto and I cross the garden toward the
hedgerow that separated the church grounds from Sylvie's house.
He was grunting his strange laugh as he pulled me along across
the wet grass.

Then he was ducking, crouching down, and shouldering his
way in among the thick undergrowth of yew trees, holly, and oak,
pulling me down to follow him. I crawled in after him, through a
green tunnel, and found myself suddenly in a kind of natural,
organic chamber, perhaps five or six feet across, four or five feet

high, where over time he had cut back the branches to form a hideout for himself. He sat on an old blanket and grinned at me. I figured I was the first person he had ever brought into this place. I smiled. "*Amigos.*"

"*Santa Maria, meua Donna.*" He got on his knees and edged up the hedge, pulling back the branches and peering through. I joined him and realized I had a perfect view of the back of Sylvie's house.

I nodded at him. "*Santa Maria, tua Donna.*" His lady. Then I made a query with my face. "Where is your treasure? *Votre tesoro?*"

He reached in among the tangle of branches and bramble behind him and, with some difficulty, pulled out a wooden box. He put it on the ground in front of me and opened it. I sat and stared and felt sick. There it was, the big bowie knife, bizarrely sealed in a large, transparent plastic bag, with traces of dry, crusted blood still visible on the blade and on the handle. Next to it, a large Sabatier kitchen knife. There was also an old photograph of a smiling black woman with a young Humberto on her knee. Carmela, I guessed. There were a couple of stones, a Christmas card, a few other bits and pieces that constituted his treasure. I looked at him.

"Who gave you the knife? *Quien ti ha dato el punhal?*"

He grinned. "*Angelo di la guarda.*"

I gave him the thumbs-up. "*Obrigado.*" He nodded and grinned back, not realizing that I was the *diavolo incarnato* who was about to turn his world upside down and inside out.

By the time we crawled back out, the CSI team had arrived. I said to Paul, "Do you own a bowie knife? Have you ever owned one?"

He frowned. "No, never. Of course not."

"Take Humberto inside. Keep him there. You and I need to talk." I looked around for a uniform. "Carter! Accompany Reverend Truelove and Humberto into the rectory. Stay with them till I get there." I looked Paul in the eye. "Stay there!"

He nodded and the three of them left. Dehan joined me and we trudged through the wet grass that was turning steadily to trampled mud, toward where the CSI team was climbing into their plastic suits at the back of their truck. There were only two of them. I knew the leader.

"Hey, Stone. How's it hangin'? Dehan."

"Hi, Phil. The real objects of interest here are the two knives. I'm curious as to why one of them is in a plastic bag, but the other isn't. If I am right, the bowie knife was used to kill Simon Martin eighteen years ago. And the Sabatier was used to kill Jacob Martin two years ago. As far as I am aware, you have samples of both of their DNA back at the lab."

"You got it. We'll run the tests for you. See if there is anything else we can find too."

"I appreciate it."

Dehan followed me then, in silence, wiping rain from her eyes, to the rectory. We found Paul and Humberto in the living room, where Paul was lighting a log fire with a match. He stood as we came in. He didn't speak, he just heaved a big sigh.

"Paul, I am not going to arrest you or Humberto right now. If the blood on the knives proves to be that of Simon and Jacob, I might."

Dehan frowned but didn't say anything.

"I could take you both into custody as material witnesses. I don't want to do that because I don't believe it is in the best interest of Humberto. So I am going to ask you to allow me to leave a police officer here until the DA decides how to proceed, once all the evidence is in. Will you agree to that?"

He nodded. "Yes. I am grateful to you, Detective."

I went on, "Paul, whatever happens next, whatever the DA decides to do, you need to start doing things right. Humberto is the victim here. He needs you. He needs you to be a father for him. Stop playing fucking Peter Pan. I am going to argue on your behalf for him to stay in your care, because I know you have risked your life for him. But." I shook my head. "It is time for you to grow up."

His face flushed. "I suppose I have earned that."

"And some. This situation cannot continue. Your son deserves more. Claim him, own up to him, either through a paternity test or by adoption. If you are afraid for your lives, talk to the Feds. We'll arrange something. But man up and get this sorted, Paul."

He nodded. "Yes. Thank you."

I turned to leave but his voice stopped me. "Detective . . ."

I stopped.

"What about Sylvie, will you tell her . . . ?"

"When there is something to tell her. We will see what the lab says."

"Yes. Of course."

IN THE CAR, the wipers set up a dreary squeak as the drizzle turned to steady rain. We moved, stopping and starting, grinding up and down through the gears, through the dense lunch-hour traffic, toward the 43rd. Whatever I had told Paul, there was no doubt in my mind what the lab was going to find, or what the DA was going to decide to do. The boxes would be ticked, and the system would kick in and take over. And that worried me, because there were questions that I wanted answered. Questions about things that, whatever way you looked at them, still did not make sense.

Dehan startled me by speaking suddenly.

"You know what the lab is going to find."

"Yeah. They are the murder weapons. There is no doubt in my mind about that."

"Then I don't understand why you haven't arrested Humberto."

I felt a sudden rush of irritation but suppressed it. "There are things that don't make much sense to me right now."

"Like what?"

I took a deep breath and tried to organize my thoughts.

"Well, to begin with, what, precisely, would make Sylvie conceal Humberto's identity as her husband's killer, even from Paul?"

She raised her eyebrows. "Even from Paul? That is odd."

"I can see her colluding with Paul, if she wanted to get rid of her husband, or if she really wanted to protect Humberto. But I can't see her witnessing Humberto murder Simon and not telling Paul. What does she gain by doing that? It doesn't make sense."

"I agree."

"Also, Humberto's account, such as it is. It's all . . . *external*."

She frowned at me, like I was crazy. "External? What do you mean?"

"It's hard to put my finger on it, but the way he describes it— it's all in his crazy language—but when he talks about it, I get the feeling he is a witness, not a participant. It's like he was outside looking through the window."

She gave a single nod. "And then there are the knives."

"Yes," I said. "Then there are the knives. How did that happen? Where did he get a bowie knife from? And what did he do? Creep over that evening, spy on her, rush in when Simon got rough with Sylvie, stab him, and then put the knife in a plastic bag to keep it with his treasure? What would make him do that?"

"And if it's some kind of fetish, why not do it with the other knife? More to the point, if he still had the bowie knife, why did he use a different knife in the first place?"

"Exactly." I sighed again and shook my head. "None of these questions is quite enough to put a hole in a prosecution, Dehan, but they make me damned uncomfortable. I want them answered." I turned onto Bruckner Boulevard. "You know? I think I'd like to talk to Mary, on her own, about her brother's murder."

She was about to answer when her phone rang. She looked at the screen. I caught the name, Saul.

She answered, "Hey, I'm at work." She was silent for a bit. Then, "Okay, seven. Yeah. You too."

She hung up.

I didn't finish, and she didn't ask what I was going to say. Five minutes later, I pulled into the parking lot, pulled out my phone, and called Sylvie's number. It rang three times before she answered.

"Mrs. Martin, this is Detective Stone. Could I talk to Mary, please?"

SIXTEEN

I opened the door, but before I got out, Dehan said, "Stone, are you mad at me?"

Cold, wet air crept in around my ankles, along with the splash and hiss of traffic in the rain. I half closed the door again.

"No, Dehan. I kind of thought you were mad at me for some reason. But, to be perfectly honest, we haven't got time for this kind of personal angst right now."

Damp streets can produce a particularly depressing kind of echo, as though the echo itself were cold and damp. Fteley Avenue produced just that kind of echo as I climbed out of the Jag and slammed the door.

I went to the toilet, dried my hair with paper, got some hot coffee, and joined Dehan at our desk. I sat and started to review the very few facts on Jacob Martin's murder. After a bit, Dehan asked, "What are you hoping to get from Mary?"

I looked up. There was something of the chastised child about her, and for a moment, that made me unreasonably angry. I dropped the file on the desk.

"I'm not sure. There are too many parallels between the two murders for it to be simple coincidence. Yet . . . ." I shrugged. "Those parallels don't seem to mean anything."

"The first and most important," she said, "is the fact that they are both . . ." She hesitated a moment. "'Martin men,' father and son, Sylvie's husband and Sylvie's son. I don't know how or why that is significant to the murders, but it is the most significant connection between them."

I nodded. "Okay, yeah . . ."

"The second, as far as I can see, is the date. So, we have two men in the same family—the only two men in the family—being killed on the same date, but sixteen years apart. Question . . ." She shrugged. "A question I can't answer right now: What makes a person kill the only two men in a family on the same date?"

"Almost like an anniversary, or a commemoration . . ."

"And then there is the position at the bottom of the stairs, and the wounds. Like a reenactment?"

"That is the obvious inference."

"But you don't like it."

I made a face and hunched my shoulders. "How does it work? Especially if we are talking about Humberto. He comes into the house and kills Simon. He runs out the door, and sixteen years later, he comes back to commemorate the first kill, but this time he brings a kitchen knife instead of a bowie knife. It just doesn't ring true. In the first place, I doubt Humberto is capable of the concept of commemoration. And then, what is so special about sixteen? It's not even Jacob's birthday."

She put her boots up on the desk and folded her hands on her belly. "There are commemorative elements in the act, but the act itself is not ritualistic enough to be a commemorative act in itself."

I thought about that. "That is very good. That is a very helpful way to look at it."

"It could be," she went on, "that something coincidental triggered the murder, and that the commemorative elements were added later, or as the murder unfolded."

I narrowed my eyes at her. "I think I follow. Give me an example."

She looked around the room, at the bustle of cops getting on with their work, carefully ignoring us. "Let's say that you take me out on a date."

I frowned.

She moved on. "I believe you are single, I really like you, and I am getting into you. And after dinner, as we are leaving the restaurant, your wife shows up and starts screaming at you. I am so mad, I pick up a bottle of, I don't know, Corison Kronos, from the table next to me and smash you over the head with it."

"Okay . . ."

"Three years and six months later, just any random period of time, I go on a date with a guy. I'm getting into him but, during the course of the evening, I discover that he is married. I am so mad that we start having a row. He gets up to leave and I see a bottle of wine on the next table. The time you did the same thing to me flashes into my mind and suddenly it seems fitting I should deal with this guy in the same way I dealt with you. So I reach for the bottle on the next table, but it's a Dalla Valle this time. Nevertheless, I hit him with it."

"So basically, you are responding spontaneously, but in a commemorative way, to a similar situation."

"Yeah."

"Using whatever comes to hand in your immediate environment."

"Mm-hm . . ."

"But there were no kitchen knives missing from the Martins' kitchen." I sat forward. "Unless . . ."

"Unless . . . ?"

My desk phone buzzed. "Mary Martin is here to see you, Detective."

"Okay. Thanks, Sergeant."

I stood. "Let's talk more about this later—" I hesitated.

She stood and sighed, and looked embarrassed.

I muttered, "Or tomorrow, or whatever."

We led Mary upstairs to interview room three and sat her at

the table. She looked nervous and kept smiling from one of us to the other. I gave her my best reassuring smile and she asked, "Will this take long? I have to help my mom with the chores."

"It shouldn't take long at all, Mary. We just need to ask you a few questions, so we can get a clearer picture of the situation."

"I don't know what I can tell you. I was only one at the time."

"Actually, it is Jacob we are interested in at the moment."

At the mention of his name she went very pale.

I watched her a moment, then added, "We think the two cases may be connected."

"Jake?"

Dehan smiled at her. "I know it's hard, Mary, but we really are trying to help you and your mom."

"How are they . . . ? How can they be . . . ?"

"We don't know." I shrugged. "It's what we need to find out. So how you can be really helpful to us, is by telling us, in as much detail as possible, exactly what happened that day."

She put her hands in her lap and stared hard at the tabletop. She was nineteen, and probably bright, but there was a fearfulness about her that suggested the emotional age of a young child.

"Gosh, it's kind of hard to remember."

Dehan spoke softly, "They were holding a fête, or a garden party, over at the church . . ."

"Yes. I remember I wasn't well. I went to bed with a chill and woke up in the morning feeling awful." She looked suddenly startled. "I mean, not so bad I couldn't go to help. I had to go and help out. We always do."

"Sure."

"So . . ." She stared down at her hands. "I guess we had breakfast, and started taking the things over."

"Things?"

"The cakes, the cookies. Mom always bakes the cakes and the cookies for the fêtes."

Dehan smiled again. "And the brownies. Those are darned good brownies."

Mary laughed. "Well, this time she forgot the brownies. That's why . . ."

She went very white.

I prompted her, "That's why . . . ?"

"That's why I had to come back for them."

"What is it about forgetting the brownies that scares you, Mary?"

"Nothing. I'm just trying to remember everything accurately."

I nodded. "Okay, we can come back to that. What happened next?"

A bead of sweat had broken out on her forehead. Her voice was unsteady. "We took all the things over to the church and started setting up the stall. And then people started arriving."

I frowned. "At what point did you realize the brownies were missing?"

She laughed. It was an impatient laugh with an edge to it. "Why are you so curious about the brownies? They are just cookies!"

"When did you realize?"

She shrugged. "I guess it must have been about eleven or half eleven."

"Where was Jacob all this while?"

"He was at home."

"So your mom called and asked him to bring them over." It was Dehan.

"No, she came and got them herself."

I scratched my chin. "She *came* and got them? I thought you went and got them, Mary."

"God!" There was an edge of hysteria to her voice now. "These brownies! They are not important!"

I frowned and smiled at the same time to show her I thought they were. "So who went to get the cookies, Mary? You or your mom?"

She took a deep breath. "Mom. Mom went to get the cookies. And then . . ."

I held up a hand. "Just before we go any further. Did Jacob ever get involved in church activities?"

She was rigid. I could see the tendons standing out on her neck, and her brow was now beaded with perspiration.

"No."

"How come? I understood that as a family you were all . . ."

"Not him."

I waited. She didn't say anything.

Dehan asked, "Since when, Mary? What made him turn away from the Lord?"

I glanced at her. It was an odd turn of phrase for Dehan, but it worked.

"When he was eleven or twelve, he started . . ." She seemed to be not so much searching for the right word, as trying not to use it. Finally, she spat out, ". . . *deviating!*"

Dehan looked startled. "Deviating? In what way?"

She closed her eyes. "Do I have to talk about this?"

"Yes, Mary." I frowned at her. "It could be very important."

"He started hanging out with . . ." Again she hesitated. "He started hanging out with non-church people at school."

"What exactly are non-church people?"

She stared hard at the wall. "People from other faiths."

I leaned forward, with my elbows on the table. "Did your mother and Paul disapprove of that?"

"Not really. Not at first."

"Not at first. So what made them change their minds?"

"He started hanging out with them after school as well. Then stopped coming to church events, stopped going to worship, and in the end, he said he was not a Christian at all."

Dehan gave her head a small twitch. "That must have been really upsetting for your mom and for Paul. How did they take it?"

"They were very upset. We all were. But there was nothing we could do about it."

"So that's why your mom went for the brownies instead of asking Jacob."

"Yes."

I drummed my fingers on the table for a moment. I had an idea taking shape in my head. "Did he have any special friends, people he used to hang out with on a regular basis?"

She nodded. "Yes, but I didn't know them."

"He must have mentioned names."

"I suppose so. I never listened."

Dehan asked the obvious question. "Mary, do you think Jacob was getting involved with a gang?"

She shook her head, then shrugged. "Probably. It wouldn't surprise me."

I said, "You and Jacob were only about a year apart. You must have been pretty close when you were small." She didn't answer, but I could see tears in her eyes. I went on. "Did that change as he got older?"

"Yes."

"He didn't talk to you? He didn't try to convince you to become an atheist . . ."

"Not an atheist."

"What, then?"

"I don't know. We never talked." Suddenly her face flushed. "I hated him! I *hated* him!"

I spoke very quietly. "What did he do to you, Mary, to make you hate him so much?"

The tears spilled from her eyes, her lip curled, and she buried her face in her hands. "He was a pig! He was a horrible pig and an animal! I hated him and detested him, and I am glad that he's dead!"

SEVENTEEN

THERE WAS A TAP AT THE DOOR AND A UNIFORMED officer put his head in. He spoke quietly.

"Detective Stone . . ."

He indicated Mary with his eyes. I put my hand on Dehan's shoulder. "You carry on. I'll be right back."

I stood and stepped out of the room into the corridor, closing the door behind me. "What is it?"

"Mrs. Martin is here. She is very upset and demanding to sit in on the interview with her daughter. She seems to believe that because it's her daughter, she has some legal right."

"Where is she?"

"I thought you might want to talk to her, so I put her in interview room five."

I nodded. "Good. Thanks, Chavez."

I stepped into room five. Sylvie half stood. Her face was taut.

"Detective Stone, I demand to see my daughter. Where is she?"

I moved toward her, talking quietly. "That's fine. We'll be done in about five minutes. I'll tell her you're here. Actually, I am glad you came in. Please . . ." I gestured at her chair. "Take a seat."

She sat back down, and I sat too.

"Mary is a very sensitive, vulnerable child. She was barely a year old when her father died."

I smiled. "She's nineteen now, Mrs. Martin. Technically she is an adult."

She shook her head vigorously. "No, no, she's not. She has always been very sensitive. She needs a lot of care and support."

"Sure. I understand, Mrs. Martin. I have a couple of questions I'd like to ask you about the day Jacob was killed."

She closed her eyes and all the color drained from her face. "Sweet Jesus, give me strength to endure these trials."

"You do remember that day, don't you?"

She nodded. "Yes, I do."

"Would you say your recollection is pretty clear and accurate?"

"Yes."

"So, here's the thing." I looked her straight in the eye. "Who went back for the brownies?"

She stared at me for a long time. "I . . . I don't . . ." She looked away, like she didn't want to see me anymore. "I don't know what you're . . ."

I spoke loudly and deliberately. "You got to the fête and you realized there were no brownies. That's right, isn't it?"

"Yes."

"Who went back for them?"

"I don't . . ." She shook her head.

"What time did you go over to the church?"

"At about nine o'clock."

"What time did you realize there were no brownies?"

She frowned, like I was an idiot. "Immediately! As soon as I started setting up the stall."

I gave a couple of exaggerated nods. "That's what I figured. So how come you waited till eleven before you went back to get them?"

She shook her head, still frowning. "I don't know. I was busy. I couldn't just . . ."

I smiled and spread my hands. "I understand. Like the day when Detective Dehan and I turned up and Mary had to tend the stall while you came to talk to us." I waited. She just stared. "It was like that, right? So why *didn't* you ask Mary to go get the brownies? She could have been there and back in two minutes. How come you waited till eleven?"

"I didn't. I mean, that's what I did. I got Mary to go."

"You sent Mary to go and get the brownies."

"Yes." She nodded.

"Or perhaps you were worried about her health. I have seen how much you care for her. So maybe you had her sit and tend the stall while you went back."

She shook her head in short, little jerks. "No."

"Because she says it was you who went back."

"No."

"But, you know? I keep wondering, why didn't you ask Jacob to bring them over?"

"He . . . I don't remember."

I leaned across the table and peered into her face, like I could open up her skull and read her mind. "What was happening, Sylvie, when you returned for the brownies? What was going on in your house?"

"Nothing!"

"Why are you lying?"

"I'm not!"

"You are both lying! Why?"

"*Stop it!*"

"What was happening in the house, Sylvie? What was going on when you went back for the brownies?"

She stood suddenly and the chair fell back with a loud clatter on the floor. "I am leaving, and you can't stop me. Where is my daughter?"

I straightened up. "We will find out, Sylvie. And you would be wise to level with us before we do." I moved to the door. "I'll go and get her."

I found Dehan outside room three, stretching her arms. As I approached, she said, "She's clammed up. She wants to go home."

"That's fine. Her mother is here to collect her."

I pushed into the room. Dehan followed. I went and leaned on the table. Mary looked up into my eyes. She looked really frightened. "Your mother says that she sent you back for the brownies, Mary. So one of you is lying. And I have to ask, what would make somebody lie about something as stupid as who went back for the brownies? I am going to give you one last chance. *What did you find in the house when you went back for the brownies?*"

Her face screwed up and she started crying again. She could barely speak, but between gasps, she said, "I didn't . . . It was Mom . . . She found him." She shook her head, biting her lip. "I was upstairs . . ."

Then Sylvie was in through the door, shouting. "Mary? Mary, honey, come to Mama!"

I turned. Mary rose and ran to her mother and they stood hugging in the doorway. She kissed her daughter's head, stroked her hair, and glared at us. "You have no call to be doing this. You found your killer. Now, for God's sake, leave us alone!"

And they left.

I heard Dehan sigh and turned to see her running her fingers through her hair. "Is she right? Are we obsessing? Are we going crazy?"

"None of those is the question, Dehan. The question is, what is making them lie about who went back for the damn brownies?"

"How do you know they are lying?"

"Because they both went pale when I asked them about it. The blood drained right out of their faces. That's a fear reflex, a reaction of the autonomic system, Dehan. It's something you can't control. Mary says Sylvie went back. Sylvie says Mary went back. One of them is lying."

She dropped onto a chair. "Okay, so they left the house about nine. According to the report, they stayed at the fête all day and returned home around four, and that was when Sylvie found Jacob's body. But now, it seems one of them returned home around eleven to get the brownies they'd left behind; and neither of them wants to admit it was them."

"That pretty much sums it up."

"Doesn't make a lot of sense."

"I know, especially as Mary wasn't even at the fête at that time."

"*What?*"

"Mary didn't go to the fête that morning."

"How the hell do you know that?"

I felt suddenly exhausted. I took a moment to gather my thoughts. "There are a couple of things. First of all, she told me she was ill . . ."

As I drew a breath to continue, Dehan's phone rang. She looked at the screen, looked at me, and sighed. She put the phone to her ear. "Yeah." She was silent a moment. "I'm at work. I can't take personal calls at work." She listened for a moment, then glanced at her watch. "Yeah, okay. Half an hour." She hung up. "I'm sorry."

"No problem."

I rose and went down the stairs to my desk. There I dropped into my chair, pulled out the Jacob file, and started to read it. A couple of minutes later, Dehan came down. She stood looking down at me. "What are you going to do?"

I looked up at her and shook my head. "I won't do much more tonight. I'll throw a steak on the barbeque and study the Jacob file."

She looked down at her boots, like she was embarrassed. I hesitated a moment, then sighed loudly.

"Look, Dehan, why not take a week or two off? The Martin case is almost wrapped up. Spend some time together, get to know each other properly, not snatching evenings while working a case. Give yourselves a chance." I shrugged. "Then, when you come back, if you still want to work the cold cases, great. Just explain to him that we have unsocial hours and he can't keep phoning you at work. If you don't, if you want to move on and do something else, well, you know I'll give you a great recommendation."

She didn't answer. She just kept staring at her boots. After a bit, I took the file and my jacket and stood. I hesitated a moment.

"You want me to pick you up in the morning?"

She shook her head. "No, thanks."

EIGHTEEN

THE RAIN HAD SETTLED IN AND DIDN'T LOOK LIKE IT
was going anywhere anytime soon. The sidewalks were spilling
people expanded to twice their size by coats, hunched shoulders,
and umbrellas, all busily, blindly jostling each other in the dying,
wet light of early evening. Shop fronts, traffic lights, streetlamps,
and headlamps were all creeping out like nocturnal predators to
sniff the rain and ease into the night.

The windshield wipers squeaked and thudded, washing away
a fractured, soaked image of an autumn evening in the Bronx,
only for another to build up, speckle by speckle, in its place.

I got home, threw the Jacob file on the table, and poured
myself a generous measure of Bushmills. I drained the glass and
poured myself another, then rummaged for steak in the fridge. I
found two. I'd bought them a couple of days back, assuming
Dehan would be coming over. She usually stayed at least two or
three times in the week, to discuss a case, sometimes to watch a
fight or a game.

She loved steak.

I smiled. One of the first things she ever told me was that she
could get intense about steak.

I put the griddle on to heat and took another slug of whiskey. In my mind's eye, I could see the church garden, the shining sun, the stall, the milling crowds, and Sylvie and Mary, both pretty and demure, with their cakes and cookies all laid out. Always together, always supporting each other, *Sylvie et Mary, contra mundum.*

But two years ago, she had not been there. What had Mary said? ". . . she came and got them herself." Mary had stayed home. I was prepared to lay money on it. Because she was sick and her mother, who cared for her so much, would not have gotten her up and out of a sickbed to help on the stall. Not unless she had a damn good reason.

My eyes slowly focused on the griddle. There was a thick column of smoke rising from it. I sprinkled coarse salt on the meat and threw it on. There was a loud hiss and the griddle caught fire. I leaned my ass on the side and watched it, feeling sour. I took another swig, reached through the flames with a large fork, and flipped the steak. Once I had scorched it on both sides, I dropped it on a plate and carried it, with the bottle of whiskey and my glass, to the table.

I cut into it, and in my mind, I followed Sylvie as she ran across the garden, dodging through the crowds, slipped through the hedge, and ran across her lawn, then in through the kitchen door . . .

What did she find there? What was happening that made her get Mary out of bed and take her to the fête? Because surely that was what had happened. There was no other explanation. Was it Jacob? Jacob's new friends? Were his pals there, giving Mary a hard time?

I stared hard at the image in my mind. There were hints, suspicions, vague ideas, but nothing concrete. Nothing solid. I stabbed the chunk of steak, stuck it in my mouth and chewed, and drained my glass and refilled it.

Fleetingly, I wondered if Dehan had put on makeup. She hadn't brought any with her. So perhaps he had taken her home to change.

I cut into the steak again and forced my mind back to Jacob. The word was there, begging for me to articulate it. Sureños. So why didn't I want to? The Sureños were not that active in that neighborhood. They were there, just like they were everywhere in the Bronx. And for sure, he would have made Latino friends at school. Did he get into a gang? Was that what was at the root of all of this? Jacob had got into a gang? That was not exactly a "different faith."

I chewed and stared at the black window with its amber speckles of rain. It looked cold and desolate. I got up to close the drapes. The traffic was gone. So were the people. There was only the cold splash of water falling from the gutter, and the liquid sheen on the blacktop, and far off the lonely tap of feet, somebody hurrying home through the rain.

I pulled the drapes closed and stood looking across the room at my plate and the bottle in the bright glare from the kitchen light.

Jacob hooking up with young Sureños made sense. It explained some things. It might explain his death. But how did it tie in with Simon? The two deaths tied in somehow. They had to. But how?

I returned to the table, sat, and cut again at my steak. I stuffed another slice in my mouth and the doorbell rang. I swallowed, took a slug of whiskey, and walked without enthusiasm to the door.

She was drenched. Her black hair was hanging in shiny rat's tails over her face. She was wearing what might have been a grin, or might equally have been a wet wince, but she was not wearing makeup. She was holding a bottle of wine in one hand and a carrier bag in the other. I stood staring at her for a moment.

"You going to let me in, or do I have to do penance out here on the stoop?"

I stood back. "No, of course not. Come in. Go up and get dry."

I looked in the bag and took the bottle to the kitchen. There were two steaks, a bottle of tequila, and a couple of lemons. I heard the shower start upstairs. I had a long glass of water, threw my burnt steak in the trash, and washed the griddle. Upstairs, I heard the shower stop, footsteps, and drawers being opened and closed in the spare bedroom. I opened the wine.

I heard her shout down the stairs, "Let me cook. I need to. It is therapeutic." There was a pause, and I heard her feet trotting down the stairs. She was toweling her hair and she had changed her clothes. "Besides, I saw you burnt the one you were eating."

"You brought a change of clothes with you?"

She shook her head. "Uh-uh. I left some here when we went to Frisco last time, looking for Tamara Gunthersen. Remember?"

"Oh."

"Did you open the wine? It's a good one. The guy said it was good. It needs to breathe."

"Dehan?"

"What?"

"Why aren't you having dinner with Saul?"

"Give me a drink, will you?"

I poured her a glass of whiskey and poured myself another. She threw the steaks on the griddle and they did not catch fire.

She sipped. "My uncle. My father's brother. He hooked me— he wanted to hook me up with his business partner's son. He is a good Jewish boy, got a great future, he's a surgeon, comes from a great family. I could do a lot worse."

I sat. "Did you like him?"

She turned her eyebrow on me. "You know, you don't *have* to talk. You don't have to ask questions. I'm coming to that."

"Okay."

"Good. So dinner one is at Uncle Ben's apartment in Manhattan. He introduces us. Polite chat. Saul's family is there. We are discreetly forced together, left alone. 'You young people must have a lot to talk about.' You know the kind of thing."

"Uh-huh."

"I told Ben, 'I am not looking for a relationship. I'm not looking to get married.' Set the table, will you? It was painful, but I got through it. But Uncle Ben won't take no for an answer, and he arranges another meal."

I got up and started setting the table. She continued talking.

"So dinner number two is also at his apartment. He says it's just informal, just me, him, and a few friends. A little get-together. The little get-together is just Ben, me, and Saul. And Ben retires early. So Saul is coming on to me. He likes me a lot, maybe we could go out sometime, get to know each other, and I am telling him I have no time, my work rules my life, yadda yadda."

"If you don't like him, couldn't you just be straight?"

"He is my uncle's partner's son. Also, I didn't *dis*like him. I just didn't want to marry him or go out with him. But I didn't want to offend him either. He's a friend of the family. So I escape and I go home. And I call Uncle Ben and I tell him to lay off. And he lays on me this whole fucking trip about family, and my dad, and don't make the same mistakes he made, I have a duty to my elders, I should marry a good Jewish boy, and when am I gonna have kids and do I wanna grow old alone and *man!*"

She dumped the steaks on a couple of plates and came out of the kitchen with them. She put them on the table. "So when he called again—Saul, that is—did I want to go out with him, I had this huge guilt complex thing that I should say yes. And suddenly, I was on this fucking road that led straight to marriage, kids, grandchildren! I was going to have dinner with him tonight and marry him in six months! And I had never even kissed the guy!"

"So what did you do?"

"He picked me up, asked me if I wanted to go and change. I told him no. He looked a bit put out. By the time we got to the restaurant I had worked through it in my head. I told him he was wasting his time. I was a fucked-up cop with a bad attitude, and he would be much better off with somebody else."

"Wow."

"There were no cabs, so I got the subway and buses, and I bought the groceries on the way. Stone?"

I smiled and said, "Yes. Welcome back."

I am not the huggy type, but that night I made an exception.

NINETEEN

I WOKE UP AT SEVEN A.M., AFTER JUST FOUR HOURS'
sleep. I had a headache that made me groan. I sat up, and after a
moment, the room caught up with me. Then, the sounds and
smells of Dehan cooking breakfast in the kitchen reached me. I
smiled and staggered to the shower.

When I got down, she put a cup of coffee on the breakfast bar
for me and said, "This is just kind of a random reaching,
clutching at straws if you will, but just assuming for a moment
that you're right . . ." She paused and pointed at me with a spatula. "And I think you are, if Jacob was hanging with the Sureños,
or some other Latino gang, and that somehow caused his death,
the one and only thing that links him with his father's death . . ."

I was nodding before she got to the end. "Is El Chato, I know.
Good morning. I was thinking that in the shower." I sipped the
coffee. It was good. Then I went over to the frying pan and
inhaled the fumes from the bacon. "Man! That is good. But
connection is putting it very strongly. The connection is that El
Chato is Latino and was a member of the Sureños."

"No." She shook her head and started spilling bacon onto two
plates with toast and fried mushrooms. "There is more." She
broke four eggs into a pan. "There is also the fact that he was

there, lurking in the garden, right by Humberto's hideout, within days of Simon's murder." She wagged the spatula at me again. "There is the fact that he is probably Humberto's *diavolo incarnato*."

"You have a point."

"Ha! I ain't just a pretty Jewish girl with no prospects of ever getting married or having kids."

"I would have to agree with that assessment." I drank more coffee as she began to slide the eggs out of the pan and onto the toast. I tried to visualize it. "So how does it work?"

She brought the plates over to the table. "You haven't set the table? Get the knives and forks, would you? And the salt. Oh, and the pepper. I have no idea how it works. El Chato is not married, and as far as I am aware, he has no kids. Not acknowledged, anyhow. He's got to be fifteen or sixteen years older than Jacob, so I don't see them hanging out together either."

I sank back in my chair and stared at her. She stared back. "What?"

I nodded. "That's it. That's the connection. It's good to have you back, Dehan. I was going crazy last night, going 'round in circles. But you just put your finger on it."

She smiled and focused on her food. "I did, huh? Like I said, not just a pretty face. Feel like sharing?"

"Nope." Suddenly, I was starving, and I attacked my plate with zest. "Humor me. I just need to confirm a couple of things. Then, if I am right, I'll share."

She raised an eyebrow but said nothing, and we ate in comfortable silence.

THE RAIN HAD STOPPED OVERNIGHT and the sky, looking freshly scrubbed, was glowing in luminous blue patches through huge white bundles of whipped cloud. I hit the ignition and pulled away.

"Is that why you said you didn't want me to pick you up, because you had made up your mind to come over?"

She angled herself in the seat to face me. "I guess. You want to know what I think?"

"Always."

"The big pain in the ass in this case is fitting all the bits together. Humberto, Paul, Brazil, Simon, Jacob, El Chato, the Church . . ."

"And there is more to come."

"Cool. So here is how I am beginning to see it . . ."

I turned onto Morris Park Avenue. The blacktop looked like washed steel, reflecting the early-morning sky.

"Paul and Sylvie were, maybe still are, lovers." She wagged a finger at me. "And I think the whole damn case hinges on that. Elizabeth said it. He's a rake. But like I said before, I think Sylvie knew how to play him, hooked him, and kept him."

"Okay."

"Now, we know that Simon does not approve of sex. Sex is for procreation and the greater glory of God. His big thing, if you'll forgive the pun, is work. So he works all the hours that God sends, plus overtime, including Sundays. Meantime, Sylvie is starting to get lonesome, and pulpit Paul is just across the garden, waiting to give her sweet consolation."

"You are beginning to sound a little lurid."

"Shut up. The inevitable happens and they start having an affair. At first they keep it together, but it starts to get out of hand, and on the Sunday in question, she is left alone, yet again, with little Mary, and Paul comes over. She already told us that she forgot to turn the lights on and get things ready for Simon that evening when he returned. Why? Because they were both tangled in blissful, postcoital bliss.

"Simon comes in, calling for her. They panic. Paul tries to escape but Simon catches them both on the stairs. Now!" She held up a hand as I turned onto Bronxdale. "Here is the interesting part where we never went before. These are both men of

God, right? You, big bad John Stone, come home and find your chick in bed with another man, you'd probably throw them both out the window. But not these guys. These guys guilt-trip each other instead. Simon, as the victim, has the moral high ground and invokes God and rails against them both, especially Sylvie, calling down fire, brimstone, and damnation on her head . . ." She paused, smiling. "But El Chato is watching all of this. Paul flees, and El Chato steps in and kills Simon."

I frowned and scratched my head. "What does El Chato gain by killing Simon?"

She spread her hands. "He burgles the house! That's why he was there in the first place, right? But while he was casing the joint, he took a fancy to Sylvie. He as much as told us that. So he kills Simon, takes whatever he wants, tells her that if she talks, Paul will most probably go down for the murder, and he, El Chato, will be back to punish her. So she feigns amnesia, he goes out the back, and, here is the smart part, he wipes the knife, puts it in a sandwich bag, and gives it to Humberto. That way, when Humberto takes it out of the bag, it will have his, Humberto's, prints on it. It implicates Humberto and, possibly, Paul. What did Humberto tell us? That the *diavolo incarnato* had killed Simon."

"Huh . . ." I made a "you might have something there" face. "Okay, so now connect it with Jacob."

She was quiet while I turned onto Bruckner Boulevard. Then she said, "Here is where it gets a bit creative, but I believe Jacob was Paul's son, and knew it."

"Wow!"

"Yeah. It is a bit of a reach, I know. But think of the timing. Then there's his character—wild, rejecting authority . . . you got to admit, he sounds like a young Paul. Maybe he went too far. Maybe he told Sylvie and Paul that he was going to blow the whistle on them. We know what that would have meant for Paul. I think Paul persuaded Sylvie to get Mary out of the house that afternoon, while he had a chat with Jacob. They had a row and he pushed him down the stairs."

"The knife?"

"The cops looked for a missing kitchen knife at the Martins' house and didn't find one. I'm willing to bet there is, or was, one missing from Paul's kitchen. How Humberto got it is less clear. Paul gave it to him? He hid it in the garden and Humberto found it . . ." She shrugged.

"Paul kills his own son."

"Wouldn't be the first time a parent killed their own child."

"That is one hell of a theory, Dehan. How do we prove it?"

She sighed. "That's tricky. Let's see what the fingerprints and blood tell us from the knives. We also need to compare Jacob's DNA with Paul's. If we can get a hit on either or both of those, maybe we can force a confession from one of them."

I pulled into the lot on Fteley Avenue outside the station and killed the engine. We sat in silence for a while, turning over her theory. She shrugged. "It's the closest we've got to a complete theory so far."

I nodded. It was.

I DIDN'T GET the call till that afternoon.

"Stone."

"Good morning, Stone. Frank here, your friendly ME." I put it on speaker as Dehan sat down. "I have some results for you. The bowie knife. The blood caked in the hilt, as expected, was a match with Simon Martin's. This *was* the knife used to kill him. Prints. There are none on the knife, but there are several on the bag. Many of them match the samples taken from Humberto, but there are others that do not."

I frowned. "Could somebody be stupid enough to wipe their prints from the weapon, put the weapon in a bag, and *leave* their prints on the bag?"

I almost heard him shrug down the phone. "That's your department, John, but I suppose if they didn't expect the bag to be kept, it's possible."

"Did you run them through IAFIS?"

"Naturally. No hits."

"Hell."

"Indeed, it must be. Now you'll have to do some detecting instead of relying on me to do your work for you. The kitchen knife. Again, as expected, the blood was Jacob's. There are prints on it, Humberto's, but here is the odd thing. They are only fingerprints."

"What do you mean?"

"Well, on the handle of a knife that has been used to stab somebody, you expect to find palm prints as well as fingerprints. But on this kitchen knife, all I can find are fingerprints, as though it had been handled with great care, and never actually gripped."

"Huh. Okay, thank you, Frank."

"Welcome. You have a good one."

Dehan was smiling. "Like I said, he was given the knives, for his treasure collection."

"He sure was."

TWENTY

It was five o'clock and there was a damp wind blowing in off the Atlantic, whipping Dehan's hair across her face. She squinted through it as she reached behind her head to tie up her hair. Beyond her, I could see the railway lines.

"You going to tell me why we're here?"

I pulled my jacket out of the back of the car and put it on, then reached in my pocket and pulled out a blank envelope I'd picked up at the precinct.

"Just humor me," I said. She followed me across the road and I rang on Ahmed's bell. There was no boisterous shouting this time. The door opened and Ahmed, dressed in jeans and a hoodie this time, tried to hide his frown behind a smile.

"Detective Stone, I am honored to see you again . . ." He looked past me at Dehan. His eyes glazed for a moment. "And this is your partner."

I returned his smile. "This is Detective Dehan, can we come in? It won't take more than a couple of minutes."

"I was just going out. But I always have time to help the police. Come in."

He showed us into the small living room where I had spoken to him before and he gestured me to a chair. I went to take off my jacket but fumbled with the envelope, like it was obstructing the sleeve. I held it out to Ahmed. "Do you mind?" He took it and I removed the jacket. "This weather, you never know if you're going to be warm or cold. Right?"

I held out my hand. He gave me back the envelope and I folded it and put it in my pocket. I sat. Dehan sat on the sofa and he sat opposite me, by the window.

"Detective, how can I help you?"

I made a small gesture of helplessness. "I am trying to understand the circumstances that led to Simon Martin's death."

He made a face of sadness and nodded. "Allah is merciful."

"So here is the thing. It is clear to us that his death, and Jacob's death sixteen years later, are in some way connected. So I was wondering two things, Ahmed: First, did you know Jacob at all? And second, how long did you continue working at the Martins' house after Simon was killed?"

"Very tragic deaths. I stop working at the church and at Sylvie's house when Simon was killed."

"Oh? Why was that?"

"Because, Allah is merciful, Mullah Al-Abas, from our mosque, advise me I should not work in Christian church. This is not correct in our religion. Sorry."

"And that happened the next day?"

He smiled and put his head on one side, placing his hands together as though in prayer. "I give her a couple of days for her grief, and meanwhile I talk to Mullah Al-Abas about what has happen. And he say to me, don't go back there no more. It is not right for a Muslim to work in a Christian church. So is coincidence, but not coincidence."

"Okay. So how about Jacob? Did you know him?"

"We see in the street, an' I say 'Hello,' and she say, 'Oh, his name is Jacob!' 'Oh, is Jewish name!'" He glanced at Dehan. "She say, 'No, no, is Bible name.' So, is many years, and often we see in the street, 'Hello! Hello!' Stopping, chatting, talk to Jacob. I see him grow into young man. Good boy. Strong. Like his father."

"Would you say that over time you and Jacob became friends, Ahmed?"

He beamed. "Yes. We become good friends. He come and visit me lots. I am like brother for him. We are good friends."

"Did his mother know that you were friends and that he was visiting you?"

He did that thing Mediterraneans do, where he pulled down the corners of his mouth and shrugged and spread his hands all at the same time. "I don't know. I never visit them. I don't see Sylvie. She is at home, in church, always. But Jacob come and visit me."

I nodded and thought for a moment. "Ahmed, did you convert Jacob to Islam?"

"Yeah. He convert to the true faith. There is but one God, and Muhammad is his prophet. Allah is merciful. I take him to see Mullah Al-Abas many times, and we are talking and Jacob is learning the true way. He is good boy."

"How old was he when this happened?"

He puffed up his cheeks and blew out, looking up at the ceiling. "I see him one day, he should be at school, but he is at the mall. I say to him, 'Hey, Jacob. Why you are no at school?' Ah! He say, 'School is stupid. I don't need school. I don't need God! I don't need nothin'!' I say, 'Woh!'" He held up his hands, laughing. "'You don' need nothing?' I ask him this. I say, 'You need food, you need drink, you need air to breathe.'" He gestured at his mouth and his nose, in case we didn't know what breathing was. "'You need light to see. Who you think give you these things? Huh?'" He laughed, creasing up his face like he had asked a really funny question. "'God! Eh? God give you these things. So, you sure you don't need God?'"

"How old would he have been when this happened, Ahmed?"

"So, maybe twelve. Young man."

"And after that he used to come to you regularly?"

"Yeah, couple times a week. We go to the mosque, talk to Mullah Al-Abas. Is very lucky for him I am meet him that day in the mall, huh?"

"Did his mother know that he had converted to Islam?"

Again he shook his head, spreading his hands. "I don't know, Detective Stone. I offer the boy the path of God, but what happen in his home, I don't know."

"Did you ever return to the Martins' home after Simon's death?"

"No, never. Is not right for me to go to that woman's home. She is not a good woman. She is a whore."

"A whore? Why do you say that?"

He shrugged and made a face of disgust. "She is no marry again. She is probably fucking Paul. Maybe other men . . ."

"You have any evidence of other men in her life?"

He shrugged. "Nah . . . People talk."

"You know she has suffered from amnesia for all these years?"

"I hear something."

"What do you think she would remember if her memory came back?"

He frowned. "I don't know . . . How I can know?"

"Because I'm thinking of bringing in a hypnotist to regress her, and then we will have a full account of what happened that night. And perhaps what happened to Jacob too."

He shrugged again. "I don't know."

I knew it was only a matter of time before Dehan opened her mouth, and now she did.

"Ahmed, let me ask you something. What is the penalty if a young man leaves the Islamic religion? What would be the penalty if Jacob decided to convert back to Christianity?"

He didn't answer her. He did a strange thing. He gave me a smile like he was asking me to be reasonable, with his head on one side, spreading his hands. "In Sharia, he must be executed. Muhammad has said that nothing, *nothing*, is so hateful in the eye of God, as an infidel. So if a man turns away from Islam, the only penalty is death. But Detective Stone, please, have some respect for my home." He gestured at Dehan without looking at her. "Don't bring filthy, Jewish whore into my house, to ask me questions. Please leave now. Get out my house."

I smiled at him. "Thanks, Ahmed. That's what I suspected." I stood. "But you know, she's not the only Jew in your house." He got to his feet and said something in Arabic that sounded obscene. I raised an eyebrow at him. "Yeah, I'm Jewish too. So you'd better watch your tongue, pal."

He made a guttural sound that was maybe going to be a word, but I cut him short. "What? You going to *spit* at me?" I laughed. "You ain't got the balls."

The result was predictable and covered most of my face. I assured him he had not seen the last of me and he screamed that he was going to report me to my superiors. Dehan and I withdrew to the car. There, I pulled an evidence bag from my pocket and, using the blade from my Swiss army knife, carefully removed the saliva from my face and put it in the bag, while Dehan watched me with narrowed eyes.

"What the hell was that all about, Stone?"

"Probably nothing. I am just covering my bases. What I need now is somewhere I can wash my face."

I started the engine and headed up toward Rhinelander Avenue.

"Since when are you Jewish?"

"I decided to convert last night when you told me about your uncle Ben, so we can marry and have fifteen kids."

She laughed noisily for a while. "You'd have to give up bacon."

"Huh. That was a short-lived conversion."

"Asshole."

I stayed on Rhinelander, headed east. After a while, she said, "I don't see how this changes anything much. I'm kind of struggling to see why you did it."

"Jacob's new friends were not Sureños. Remember, Mary said they were from a non-Christian faith."

"Oh." She thought about it a bit, then scowled at me. "Shit!"

I turned into Seminole Avenue and pulled up in the parking

lot of the Jacobi Hospital. We rode the elevator and found Frank in his lab. He looked surprised to see us. I pulled the plastic evidence bag and the envelope from my pocket and showed them to him.

"Frank, what do I need to do to get you to do this today? Name it. Whatever it is, I'll do it."

He frowned. "Why is it so important?"

"Because it involves the murder of a child, and there could be other lives at stake."

"Jacob Martin?"

I nodded.

He sighed. "Every case I have is a priority, John. You know that. Every one of them involves somebody's life, somebody's loved one."

"I know. And you know I wouldn't ask you if it wasn't really important. It's a clean sample. I know you can do this in eight hours. The prints in less. The clock is ticking on this one."

He sighed. "Leave it on my desk. I'll get to it as soon as I can."

I went into the small cubicle of his office, found a scrap of paper, and jotted down exactly what I wanted. Then I found a paper clip and stuck it to the envelope and the bag. I didn't leave them on his desk. I took them and put them in his hand.

"I owe you. If you ever want to use my place in Florida, or the boat, you only have to ask."

His eyebrows shot up. "You have a boat and a place in Florida?"

"No. But if I ever have, they are yours for the asking."

Dehan was leaning on the doorjamb. She shook her head at Frank. "I told him already today. He's an asshole."

TWENTY-ONE

WE STEPPED OUT INTO THE FADING EVENING SUNSHINE.
There were expanding patches of dark blue sky above. I looked up
at the dissipating clouds, but in my mind, I was struggling to fit all
the pieces of the puzzle together. It was like doing a jigsaw blind-
folded in a dense fog. There were no dissipating clouds there. I
walked toward my car, thinking about what I had asked Frank to
do. I was pretty sure what the answers would be, and I was
wondering about the implications. I heard Dehan's voice
behind me.

"Okay Stone, you need to stop." I did. I stopped and turned
to frown at her. She spread her hands. "Clue me in, Sensei! I feel
like I'm tagging along for the ride!"

I looked at my watch. It was not too early for supper. "Yeah.
Let's grab some food and a beer and I'll share my thoughts with
you."

"Jeez, boss! Thanks!"

"There's a pizza place near here. You like pizza."

"Yeah. I like pizza. I like being kept in the loop more."

We climbed in the car and pulled out of the lot. All the way
down Seminole Avenue and half the way down Morris Park, she
stared at me, and I tried to articulate my thoughts. Finally, I

pulled up outside Patsy's Pizzeria, we went inside, and I ordered two pepperoni pizzas and two beers.

We sat at a table by the window with a red gingham tablecloth and a small vase of flowers on it. She took a pull of her beer, leaving herself a white mustache on her upper lip, which she wiped away with the back of her hand.

"I haven't worked it out, Dehan. But I have a gut feeling."

"So tell me."

I sighed. "Okay, so the first thing is, we know that the bowie knife was the weapon used to kill Simon Martin. Agreed?"

"Sure."

"Okay, now we know that Humberto handled the bag, and so did somebody else. But there are no prints on the knife."

"Sure, but we were already speculating that El Chato could have killed Simon and given the knife, in the bag, to Humberto."

I spread my hands and leaned back to allow Patsy to deliver the two pizzas. She smiled at us. "Enjoy!"

When she'd gone, I said to Dehan, "But the second set of prints, the ones that are *not* Humberto's, are not in IAFIS."

She stopped with her knife halfway to the pizza. "Oh . . . And they would be if they were El Chato's."

"Precisely. And the kitchen knife, which we now know was used to kill Jacob, has Humberto's prints, but fingerprints, not palm prints, and made *postmortem*! As though he had been handling the knife with great care, after it had been wiped. Like it was part of his treasure collection."

She nodded repeatedly as she cut her pizza into twelve almost manageable slices. "And you are thinking, who knew Humberto well enough to know he would take the knives as part of his treasure, and so incriminate himself? And who might be in a position for Humberto to see them in the garden . . . ?"

We both bit into our pizzas and sat staring at each other and chewing. I swallowed and drank while she bit again. I said, "I am not clear yet, Dehan. That is, I am clear that Humberto is not the guy, and I am clear El Chato is not the guy. But I am not clear about Paul, Mary, Sylvie, or Ahmed. They are all tied up in a kind of spaghetti mess, and I am trying to understand each one of them, what their motivations are . . ."

She frowned. "But Ahmed? The guy's a creep, but I don't see what motive he would have."

I did a little side-to-side dance with my head. "I don't know . . ."

"Unless Paul and Sylvie had persuaded Jacob to come back to the fold, and it was a simple fatwa."

"It's within the bounds of possibility, Dehan. But what about Simon?"

She made a face like she wasn't believing her own words. "He blasphemed against Allah?"

"It's also possible, but it fails to explain why Sylvie would refuse to name him and pretend to have amnesia."

"*Man!* This is like one of those damn Chinese puzzles. You get one bit, but then you can't get the other!" She scowled at me. "Son of a bitch! You think you've got it, don't you?"

I sighed. "There is one scenario that could, possibly, explain everything. But it's a reach."

"So tell me!"

"I'm not sure . . ." As I said it, my phone rang. I picked it up and answered, "Stone."

I stood as I listened. I signaled Dehan with my head to get up and pay as I headed for the door. "Okay, we're on our way."

Dehan joined me as I was climbing into the car. The sun had gone down and the light was fading. I slammed the door and fired up the engine. She got in beside me and I took off.

"There's been an attack at the Martins'. There are two units on their way. There was an intruder in the house. It's not clear if anyone was hurt. Sylvie and Mary were apparently both pretty incoherent. Bogart is just a block and a half on the left."

I took the corner at fifty, which the old Jag did with cool elegance, and hammered the big four-liter engine down another block and a half to Sylvie's house. There I skidded to a halt. As we got out, I could hear the sirens of the approaching patrol cars. Dehan ran up the five stairs of the stoop as the door opened. Warm light flooded out and Mary stood silhouetted in the doorway.

"Thank God you're here! Mom is in the living room."

I ran up the stairs and followed Dehan in. Sylvie was sitting on the sofa. She was bent forward, sobbing into her hands and occasionally wailing with grief. The French doors were open onto the garden. At a glance, I could see one of the panes of glass was broken. I turned to Mary. She was trembling.

"What happened?"

"There was a man in the house."

"He escaped?"

She nodded and pointed at the French doors.

"How long ago?"

"Five, ten minutes."

I could hear the sirens of the patrol cars pulling up outside. I turned to Dehan. "Go out. Organize a search of the area. I'll get the statements."

She left to meet the cars. I pointed to the sofa. "Sit down, Mary. Are either of you hurt?"

She shook her head.

"Tell me what happened."

"We'd been at Paul's . . . at Reverend Truelove's. Mom had been cleaning in the church and I was helping at the rectory. I guess we'd been there an hour or so when Mom came in. She didn't look well. She's been real stressed lately. She asked the reverend if he had an aspirin, because she had a bad headache. He fetched her one himself and told her she should go home and lie down. They argued for a bit, but he insisted, and finally she left."

"Who else was there while all this was happening, Mary?"

"Just the police sergeant you left there."

"Where was Humberto?"

"Well, he was around. He's always around somewhere. But I couldn't tell you exactly where."

"So what happened next?"

"Well, I finished up a couple of chores, and then the reverend told me I should leave the rest and go home to look after Mom."

"So you went home."

"Yes, I did."

"Mary, do you and your mom always use the gap in the hedge in the garden?"

She smiled. "Why, yes. We all do . . ."

Sylvie slowly raised her tear-drenched face and looked at me.

I met her gaze, and after a moment I asked her, "How are you feeling?"

Her face was bitter. "How do you think? I told you to leave it alone."

"I can't do that, Sylvie. You know I can't." I smiled at Mary. "Why don't you make your mom some tea, Mary?"

She nodded and went out to the kitchen. Sylvie watched her leave, then said, "You are going to bring disaster on us all."

"That's not my purpose, Sylvie. My purpose is to find the truth and, if necessary, bring the killers to justice. But if you and Paul keep getting in the way, maybe there will be a disaster."

"God has his own justice."

"Maybe so. Are you going to tell me what happened?"

She sighed and closed her eyes, then flopped back on the sofa. "I went upstairs to lie down in the dark. I started drifting off to sleep. I don't know how long I was like that. Next thing, I heard a noise. I'm not sure what it was. Like a bang or something. Then the French windows opened and closed. I assumed it was Mary come home from Paul's. Shortly after that, I heard feet climbing the stairs . . ."

Her face started to contort and tears spilled from her eyes again. She raised her fingers to her mouth. When she spoke, her voice was high-pitched, almost strangled.

"Oh God, help me! I thought the steps sounded heavy. It wasn't like Mary. I thought maybe Paul . . ." She sat forward again, convulsing. Her eyes were wide and staring. "The door opened and he just stood there, staring at me."

"Who did? Did you recognize him?"

She stared at me like I had asked some insane question. "No. The lights were off. And he had a kind of hood over his face." She shuddered and covered her face with her hands. I thought she was going to turn hysterical, but she said, "He just rushed at me, without a word. He just rushed, and I saw he had a huge knife in his hand. I screamed."

She looked at me suddenly, as though I might disapprove of her screaming.

I said, "Okay, you're doing great, Sylvie. This is really helpful. Now I need you to think carefully before you answer. Did he say anything, anything at all?"

She shook her head. "No. He just made a horrible noise, like an animal. And when I saw the knife, I started screaming." She shuddered again. "I must have jumped off the bed. I saw his knife rip at the quilt where I'd been lying."

"What kind of knife was it, Sylvie?"

She froze, and her eyes locked onto mine. She took a long moment to answer. "The same. The same kind of knife."

"The same as . . . ?"

"The same as the one he used to kill Simon."

"Was it the same man?"

She covered her mouth and spoke through sobs. "I don't know. I don't know. I was so scared. I thought . . ."

Mary came in with a cup of tea. Sylvie reached for it with trembling hands. Mary glanced at me. "Detective, can I get you some tea or coffee?"

I shook my head. "No, thanks, Mary. Sit down, would you. Tell me what you remember. What happened when you got back?"

She pointed at the French doors. "I was coming across the garden, and I saw the French windows were open. So I went toward them, thinking I could come in that way and close them from the inside. But as I got closer, I realized the glass was broken. So I hurried over to see what had happened. And as I opened them wide, that's when I heard the screaming upstairs." She looked at her mother, as though seeking confirmation. "I could hear her screaming for help. She just kept screaming, 'Help, somebody help me.'"

I turned to Sylvie. "Did he hurt you with the knife?"

The question seemed to confuse her for a moment. "I don't think so. I don't think I'm bleeding."

"What happened next, Sylvie?"

Her face contracted at the memory, and she hunched her shoulders. "He jumped on the bed. I thought he was going to kill me. I ran. I don't know where. I just ran, screaming. I think he grabbed me and threw me. I thought I was going to die. I kept feeling the knife about to stab me, all over my body."

"What did you do, Mary?"

Now she looked scared. "I don't know if I did wrong, Detective. But I heard Mom screaming for help, and all the crashing and tramping around upstairs. So I grabbed a knife from the kitchen and ran to help her. I didn't think. I just acted from instinct."

"That's fine. So you ran up the stairs . . . ?"

"I ran up the stairs. Mom's door was open. I rushed in and I saw Mom on the floor by the bed and this man bending over her, and he had a big knife raised up in his hand, like he was about to stab her with it."

"What kind of knife was it?"

"It was like one of those big hunting knives."

"What happened next?"

Mary's eyes flooded, but she kept her composure. She put her arms around her mother and held her. "I don't know if I did the wrong thing, but I rushed at him and I slashed at him with the kitchen knife, screaming at him to leave my momma alone."

"You were defending your home and your family. You were perfectly entitled to do what you did. But I need to know, did you injure him? Did you stab him? It could really help us identify the man."

She thought about it. "Yeah. I am pretty sure I did. Maybe on his shoulder or his right arm."

Sudden shouts and the sound of scrambling made me turn and stand and go to the French doors. Evening was turning to night, and there were flashlights dancing at the end of the garden. A voice shouted, "*Don't move!*"

There was the sound of scuffling and scrambling. Then Dehan's voice, authoritative and calming.

"Okay! Take it easy! I'm not going to hurt you." There was a pause. Then her voice again. "Stone? Is that you?"

"Yeah."

I could make out a small group of people walking toward me. Dehan's voice spoke again. "It is Humberto. He was hiding in the bushes. He seems to be hurt."

TWENTY-TWO

IT WAS AN ODD TABLEAU. SYLVIE AND MARY SITTING and holding each other on the sofa, staring at Humberto, who was looking huge and miserable between two uniformed cops, with Dehan standing beside him, rubbing her hand like it hurt. I went over to him. As I approached, he seemed to cower and wince.

I smiled. "*Amigo.*"

He smiled back, but uncertainly. "*Meu amigo.*"

"Are you hurt, Humberto?" I struggled to remember my schoolboy Latin. "*Injuria, doleo, malum?*"

He nodded his massive head and looked at Sylvie. "*Diavolo malefico feto injuria mina Donna.*"

I turned to Dehan. "You okay?" She nodded. "Call Paul, will you? Get him over here."

She pulled out her phone and stepped into the hall. I reached over and turned Humberto gently around. "Where are you hurt, Humberto?"

I took hold of his hands and saw his right one was thick with blood. I pointed to it and looked into his face. "*Injuria.*"

He pouted. "*Diavolo malefico.*"

I examined the sleeve and found the slash on his lower arm,

just below his elbow. I turned and called, "Dehan. We need an ambulance too."

She stepped back into the room. "I already called them. Paul is on his way."

"Did you find a weapon?"

"Not yet. Jones and Hanson are looking."

"Sylvie, is this the man who attacked you?"

Mary was frowning at her. Sylvie bit her lip and the tears started to spill again. "It might be. I am not sure."

"Mary? Is this the man who was attacking your mother?"

Humberto was looking confused, from Sylvie to me. He said, "*None feto malo. None feto malo.*"

"Mary?"

"I don't think so . . ." She turned to her mother, but her mother had her eyes closed and was sobbing again. Mary looked back at me. "I'm not sure."

"Where is the knife you used?"

She half stood. "Oh, it's on the floor in Mom's room. Should I go and . . . ?"

"No. Just leave it where it is. Dehan, we'd better get a CSI team here."

"On their way, Sensei."

There was a footfall at the French windows and Paul stepped in. He scowled around the room. "What in the name of God is going on?"

"Sit down, Paul. That is what we are here to find out. Please, none of you leave this room. We'll be back in a moment. Dehan, let's take a look upstairs."

I put one of the officers on the front door and left the other to stand watch over Sylvie and Paul, and Dehan and I climbed the stairs to the bedroom. The bed was rumpled, as you'd expect after somebody had slept on it and then jumped on it. The lamp on the near bedside table was knocked over, presumably from where Sylvie had been thrown against it, and, on closer inspection, there was an area of the quilt that had been slashed.

Dehan had hunkered down and was looking at a large kitchen knife that lay on the carpet. There was a substantial amount of blood on the blade. She spoke as though to herself.

"Brave girl."

I nodded. "That is the blood of our killer."

She looked up at me. "You think it was Humberto after all?"

There was the sound of a siren outside, and after a moment, the door opened. I went down the stairs to meet the paramedics and pointed them in the direction of the living room. The CSI team was close behind them. I greeted Luis, the team leader, and pointed up the stairs.

"In the master bedroom. There is a knife. The blood on the blade is a top priority. It belongs to the assailant who just attempted to murder the owner of the house. The prints on the handle belong to the owner's daughter, so you'll want her prints for comparison."

"Gotcha."

"The assailant escaped through the back garden. I have two officers out there now, but we are going to need to go over it with a fine-tooth comb."

He gave me the thumbs-up and made his way upstairs with his team. We returned to the living room, where a paramedic was bandaging Humberto's arm. Paul was on the sofa next to Sylvie with his arm around her. He looked at me with bitterness in his face.

"You see what you've done, Detective? You couldn't leave things alone . . ."

"Can it, Paul. I'm sick of hearing that crap. We don't leave murders uninvestigated just because it happens to suit you and Sylvie to ignore them. Are we clear on that?"

He muttered something and turned back to Sylvie.

"I need to know what happened to Humberto. I need to know what he saw in the garden. Can you ask him? Can you make any sense of his answers?"

He turned to Humberto and spoke to him in Portuguese. Humberto's face took on a look of awe and horror.

"*Santa Maria plena di graza, aclamando auxilio, deu! Deu! Auxilio! El diavolo incarnato com punhal sanguino mi atacato o jardam. Eu lo abatido il suo punhal. Humberto luta! Luta! E il diavolo corre! Corre!*"

Suddenly, he was laughing his braying laugh and bouncing up and down. The paramedic turned to me.

"Detective, he should really go to the hospital."

I nodded and looked at Paul. "What did he say?"

He sighed. "It doesn't make a lot of sense. He says that Sylvie was screaming for help. He equates her with the Virgin Mary. There was a devil incarnate with a dagger that attacked him in the garden. He defeated the devil and knocked the dagger from his hand. They fought and the devil fled."

"He knocked the dagger from the devil's hand?"

"That's what he says, but it could all be a fantasy."

"Yeah, you said that before about him. Maybe if you listened more and judged less, Paul, you might learn something about your son."

"I don't need to take that from you, Detective."

"No, you don't, but you'd be wise to. You want to go to the hospital with him?"

"Yes."

"There will be an officer with you. Paul, Humberto is not a suspect in this investigation, and I am trying really hard to keep you and Sylvie from the top of my list. My advice to you is stop trying to hide things from me, quit this stupid conspiracy of silence, stop behaving like you're guilty. Don't screw it up."

He got up and they left with the ambulance crew.

When they'd gone, I sat and watched Sylvie a moment. She was quiet, leaning against her daughter.

"Sylvie, I hope you've been doing some thinking. Because all your efforts to keep what happened a secret have been to no avail. All you've done is delay things, and in delaying them, made them worse. You could have been killed today, and it was only the courage of your daughter that saved your life. But I hope you realize that in saving you, she put her own life at risk. You are damned lucky that today you are not the mother of two dead children."

She closed her eyes and seemed to shiver. Mary looked at me in horror. I pressed on. "Sooner or later you have to confront the truth, Sylvie. Sooner or later you will have no choice but to face up to the reality. You may as well do it now, because the longer you delay, the tougher it's going to be."

In my peripheral vision, I sensed Dehan sit in the armchair. She was watching me as hard as she was watching Sylvie.

"Sylvie, look at me."

She opened her eyes and looked at me. There was resentment, and maybe even hatred in her eyes.

"Did Humberto attack you tonight?"

It was barely perceptible, but she shook her head.

"Do you know who did attack you? Did you recognize your attacker?"

She closed her eyes and turned away from me. She was not going to talk.

Behind me, the French doors opened and an officer put his head in. "Detective, we found a knife."

I turned to Dehan. She was frowning. I smiled. I said to the uniform, "Go upstairs and inform the CSI team leader, will you?"

To Dehan, I said, "Let's take a look."

We stepped out into the garden. Thirty or forty feet away, we could see the glow of a flashlight, and we made our way toward it. As we got closer, we could see there was a circular patch of grass illuminated by the torch, and at its center there was a large hunting knife with a rubber grip and a serrated back to the blade.

We hunkered down to look at it. Dehan said, "He obviously likes this kind of knife. But two gets you twenty he was wearing gloves."

I nodded. "You can count on it. But my bet is he ain't the

brightest button in the sewing box, and he only wore gloves today. My bet, he's owned this knife for a long time, and it is covered in his prints."

She looked at me and laughed. "You're kidding."

"I'll bet you a steak dinner."

"You're on."

TWENTY-THREE

FRANK PHONED WHILE LUIS WAS BAGGING THE KNIFE.

"John, I rushed the tests for you, and I have the preliminary results. God alone knows how you arrived at that conclusion, but you were right."

"About the prints or the DNA?"

"Both. It was exactly as you thought . . ."

I nodded, even though he couldn't see me. There was a large, orange moon rising over the treetops in the east. I smiled at Dehan. I think she smiled back and winked. "That makes perfect sense, then. Listen, Luis is coming in in a while with a couple of knives that were used in an attack here at the Martins' home."

"Another one?"

"Yeah. It seems I stirred up a hornets' nest. Will you acquaint him with your findings? They'll be relevant."

He was silent for a moment, then sighed like he wanted to kick himself. "You want me to look at the knives? I can do it on my own time."

"I would appreciate that, Frank, though I have a hunch we'll have this sewn up tonight."

"You better start house hunting in Florida, pal!"

I hung up and grinned at Dehan. "You haven't got any hot dates tonight, have you?"

She looked surprised. "What do you call this?"

I barked a laugh and called the captain. He answered like I was his least favorite mother-in-law.

"John! You just caught me. I was on my way home."

"Captain. I need an APB on Ahmed Abadi." I outlined the situation and told him we were headed to Ahmed's house and would need backup. "He may be on the run, and he may be armed, injured, and very dangerous."

"I'll see to it. Keep me posted . . . or, um, report to me in the morning."

"Will do, sir, in the morning."

"Good."

I hung up and hesitated a moment. "Dehan, I'll meet you at the car. There's just something I want to look at in the rectory."

She didn't look happy. She sighed and made her way toward the Martins' house, and I headed through the fence toward the rectory. There, in the kitchen, I found what I had expected to find. Another piece slotted into the puzzle.

On the way back, I instructed one of the patrol cars to stay with the Martins till the morning, then stepped into the street. It was quiet, and there was a chill in the air. The red-and-blue lights from the patrol cars pulsed, silent on the blacktop. The amber glow from the streetlamps was diffused by the leaves of the plane trees, making the road into an eerie tunnel of half-resolved shadows.

I climbed into the muffled seclusion of the Jaguar and closed the door. Dehan got in beside me. Her door echoed like a single shot in the night.

"Okay, Stone, time to talk. I am not here to tag along. I'm your partner. You seem real convinced of whatever it is you think, and so far you've been right. But I am not seeing it. Explain."

I fired up the engine and headed north up Bogart Avenue, fast.

"Would you be mad if I said I wasn't sure myself?"

I made the tires squeal as I turned left out of Bogart onto Morris Park and accelerated toward Bronxdale. She looked at me like I was insane.

"Yes?"

I winced. "It's a case of elimination, Dehan. It couldn't *be* anybody else, could it? You know the old Holmesian adage, 'Eliminate the impossible . . .'"

"'And whatever is left is the truth,' I know. But . . ." She spread her hands.

I went on, "Exactly, whatever is left is the truth. Therefore, it had to be Ahmed, because it *couldn't* be anybody else. Once I accepted that, things began to fall into place. But there are still a couple of details I need to confirm."

"Like?"

I made a right on Bronxdale and hit the gas, moving north at speed toward Rhinelander. Somewhere in the night, I could hear the wail of sirens, our backup coming to join us. I grabbed the radio.

"Dispatch, this is Detective Stone proceeding to the residence of Ahmed Abadi on Unionport Road. I am approaching from Rhinelander Avenue. Requesting backup approach from Morris Park."

The radio crackled its confirmation and relayed the message.

The tires squealed as I made a left onto Rhinelander. I hit the gas and we surged forward and covered the half mile to Unionport Road in thirty seconds. As we moved down the road, I could feel the adrenaline pumping hot in my belly.

"We don't know what weapons he has at home, Dehan. We do know he is prepared to kill and he is reckless. Remove the safety on your automatic, and if you have to use lethal force, do not hesitate. Are we clear?"

She eyed me a moment. "Yeah, we're clear."

I pulled into Unionport and stopped forty feet from his house, placing my car across the road. I got out, drew my weapon, and removed the safety. I could hear my backup approaching along Morris Park Avenue, a thin wail above the whine of a turbine on the railway tracks.

Two patrol cars pulled into the road ahead of me. One blocked the road. The other pulled up to the door. Two uniformed cops got out. I knew them, Stuart and Chen. I approached them.

"Hold your positions here at the car. He may be armed and he is very dangerous. Stay behind your vehicle."

They acknowledged, drew their weapons, and remained behind the car. I climbed the two stairs to the door and hammered loudly on it, then leaned on the bell. I could hear a woman screaming hysterically inside. She seemed to be saying something, but not in English. I hammered again.

"*NYPD! Open up!*"

The screaming grew closer. We backed up and stepped to the side, training our weapons on the door. It was wrenched open by a woman encased from head to foot in a black burka, like a Victorian ghost who's just come down the chimney, covered in soot. She was screaming and waving her hands, and behind her she had four very frightened-looking kids.

We moved toward her, keeping her covered. I said, "Where is Ahmed? Ahmed Abadi? Where is he?"

She just kept shouting at me, waving her hands around. She sounded as though she was appealing to me for sympathy or understanding. Both were impossible right then. I turned toward the patrol car.

"Stuart! I need this woman and her kids taken into custody as material witnesses. Get a translator too. She's speaking Iraqi. It is very urgent."

"Yes, sir!"

Chen made the call while Stuart took her and the kids and put them in the back of the vehicle, to await the translator and further backup. Dehan and I went inside. She covered the stairs while I kicked in the living room door.

"Clear!"

The kitchen was also clear, and we moved up the stairs to the bedrooms. The bathroom was empty, but there was a blood-stained towel and shirt in the bath. A small room with four beds in it was also empty. The next room was obviously his and his wife's. The wardrobe was open, and there was a suitcase on the bed. In it, there was a pump-action shotgun, a Sig P226 TacOps automatic pistol, and several boxes of ammunition. Dehan pointed to one of the boxes. I had already seen it. It was empty.

"Those are intermediate cartridges. They are not for a pistol. You'd use them in an assault rifle."

We stared at each other, like we were reading each other's minds.

"Where has he gone, Dehan?" I turned and ran down the stairs.

"Stuart! Where are you?"

"Detective?"

He was at the door.

"Get the captain. I don't give a damn where he is or what he's doing. Get him. Inform him we have a situation. Ahmed Abadi is at large and injured, armed with an assault rifle. Call Dispatch. I want an armed guard on the Martins' house and on St. George's Church. Also, we *need* a translator *now!*" I pointed at the patrol car. "I don't give a damn what you do or what the Geneva Convention has to say about it. I assume full responsibility. Make that woman tell you where her husband has gone. *Now!*"

But I knew it was pointless. I knew we were out of time. I turned. Dehan was behind me.

"Where did he go, Dehan?"

"The mosque. It's just up the road."

I nodded. "Yes. The mosque. Let's go."

We climbed in the Jag and I swung back toward Rhinelander Avenue.

"This is going to get damned complicated. We cannot let this get political."

Dehan looked grim. "Good luck with that. I think it's too late. I think it already did."

I glanced at her. I knew she was right. "Then we have to take this son of a bitch down before the politicos get here."

She looked at me, but she didn't say anything. I pulled up outside the mosque and climbed out.

It didn't look like you'd expect a mosque to look. There were no minarets and no domes. It was just two shabby, terraced houses, one painted a dull yellow, and the other a faded oxblood. The doors and windows were open, and there was a guy in a robe with a big beard leaning on the wall outside, watching us with his arms crossed. I approached him and showed him my badge.

"Detectives Stone and Dehan. I'm looking for Ahmed Abadi. You know where he is?"

He hunched his shoulders slightly, but that was all he responded with.

I did it as quickly and quietly as I could. I weigh two hundred and twenty pounds and there isn't much fat on me. I put my whole weight behind the punch and drove my fist deep into his solar plexus. As he doubled up, we both grabbed him and dragged him inside. Dehan was speaking urgently.

"This man is ill! Make way! Get a doctor!"

There were not many people inside, just a couple of young guys and an old man with a beard down to his waist. Dehan closed the doors, and I threw the guy with the hat across a coffee table with a bunch of magazines and leaflets on it. Dehan pulled her piece, and I took a moment to look at the two young guys. One had scared eyes, the other looked terrified. I grabbed the terrified one and dragged him to where his pal had rolled onto the floor, vomiting. Tripped him up so he fell on his back on top of his friend. I knelt on his chest and shoved the barrel of my 9mm into his mouth. I knew I was screwed, and I knew my career was probably over. But it was a small price to pay to stop a crazy man with an assault rifle. I didn't care what damned religion he was. He had to be stopped. I let him see that in my eyes, then snarled.

"I am going to count to three. Then I am going to blow your kneecaps off. Then I am going to find your mother and your sisters, and I am going to blow their kneecaps off too. You understand me? Now, where is Ahmed Abadi? One, two . . ."

He was already gagging and babbling.

"He is no here! No here!

"*Where?*"

"He is making jihad!"

I gave him a backhander that made his eyes water. "*Where, goddamn it? Where?*"

The old guy with the long beard started babbling. "Please, sir! Please! We are not fundamentalist! We just want peace! Please no hurt! Ahmed is acting on his own! He been here talking crazy. We no support him!"

I growled, "I gave you your chance. You blew it!" I rammed the Glock against his right kneecap and he screamed like a girl.

"*No! No! No!*"

I gave him another backhander. "For the last time! Where?"

They all started shouting at the same time. And they all shouted the same thing.

"*The whore! The whore and the priest! The whore and the priest!*"

TWENTY-FOUR

DEHAN CALLED FOR FURTHER BACKUP TO MEET US AT the Martins' while I burned rubber back down Rhinelander and Bronxdale. On the way, the captain called. I put him on speaker.

"What the hell is going on, Stone?"

"We have a situation, sir. The politics are up to you. I have a dangerous man armed with an assault rifle. He is headed for the Martins' home and for St. George's Church. I am told he is on a jihad. We have every reason to believe he is going there with murderous intent. It is my intention to stop him before anybody else gets hurt."

"Stone, the ramifications . . ."

"Sir, with all due respect, that is your department. I think you need to contact the local community leaders and make them understand that killing people and harboring murderers is against the law."

"You don't need to tell me my job, Stone. Listen to me. Isn't Dehan . . . um . . . could there be a conflict of . . . um . . ."

"Breaking up, sir. We are at destination and facing imminent threat. Over."

I pulled up outside St. George's on Fowler Avenue, muted my cell, and got out. It was deathly quiet, and there was nobody visible in the street. We moved quickly to the side of the road, seeking the cover of the trees in the church garden and the parked cars. We came to the gate and squatted down.

I peered in and saw the lights in the rectory all seemed to be turned off. I wondered if Paul and Humberto were still at the hospital. The church looked massive and strangely ominous in the dull, orange light from the street. I slipped into the garden, indicating to Dehan I would take the left path between the rectory and the nave, and she should take the right path, by the old graveyard. We split up and sprinted for the church.

The narrow passage under the canopy of trees became a blind, claustrophobic tunnel of black shadows against even blacker depths. The only light came from a dim circle of moon-glow on the lawn up ahead. I could hear my own breath and my heartbeat, magnified in the darkness. I moved forward inch by inch, with my flesh expecting the plunge of a blade or the shattering shock of a bullet at any second.

I made it to the end of the nave and stepped into the moonlight, keeping close against the wall. Then I slipped around the church tower, looking for Dehan. She wasn't there. I cursed silently and slid a little farther around, to peer down toward the gravestones. That was when I felt the cold, hard pressure of a gun barrel between my shoulder blades and heard a cool, steady voice in my ear: "Freeze, motherfucker . . . Oh, it's you. All clear this side."

I turned to look at her. She was giggling like a schoolkid. I told myself people deal with stress in different ways, and we moved on across the lawn to the back of the house. I had left two patrolmen to guard the Martins' house, but I guessed they were on the inside. We had backup coming, to cover the front and back of the house, but it hadn't arrived yet. The 43rd was stretched at the best of times. Tonight they'd be stretched real thin.

Dehan moved up to the kitchen door, and I slipped over to the French windows. They hadn't pulled the drapes yet, and I could see Sylvie lying on the sofa, with her head on Mary's lap.

She had put on a heavy, woolen cardigan and was clutching it up to her mouth. Paul was in one of the armchairs, staring silently at Sylvie, and Humberto was in the other chair, looking really depressed. Obviously, they'd been given the all clear. I looked over at Dehan. She was squatting down by the step and signaled me to join her. As I approached, she pointed at the door. It was about an inch open.

I mouthed, "Cover me . . ."

She gave a single nod and trained her gun on the center of the doorway. I flattened myself against the wall and with the tips of my fingers gently pushed the door. It swung back a couple of feet and came to a stop. I inched closer and pushed again. It wouldn't move. It had come up against something solid on the other side. I pushed harder. It gave a little, but softly sprang back when I let go. I knew what it was, and when I glanced at Dehan, her face told me she knew what it was too.

I put my shoulder to the panel and heaved silently, then squeezed in through the gap. The cop on the floor had been with the department for just over a year. I knelt to feel his pulse. He didn't have one, and the dark pool on the floor told me why. For a moment, I felt ashamed that I didn't remember his name.

I stood and moved to the door that gave onto the dining room. It was open. The lights were off, but I had a clear view to the living room. I could hear the faint murmur of Paul's voice. It had lost that bombastic, sermonizing sound I had heard before. It was more subdued. I took three silent strides to the entrance to the hallway and waited in the shadows. Dehan came up behind me.

I was about to move into the hall when I heard movement and froze. There were two heavy steps, and a large body came into view. It paused a moment and kicked the living room door in. I heard Mary and Sylvie scream, and next thing, there was a hysterical male voice screaming over the top of them. I recognized the voice as Ahmed's.

I didn't wait. I ran. Dehan was close on my heels. I burst

through the door. Ahmed was standing over Sylvie. She was cowering, screaming hysterically, and Mary was lying over her, trying to protect her with her own body. For a moment, everything seemed to happen in slow motion. I saw Ahmed holding a Heckler & Koch assault rifle at his shoulder, pointing the muzzle down at Sylvie. I saw Humberto gaping up at him, and I saw Paul staring in disbelief. I had my automatic aimed at the back of Ahmed's head and I was yelling at him to drop his weapon and get on the floor. He was so hysterical I am not sure he even heard me.

I knew that if I shot him in the back of the neck, it would sever his spinal cord and paralyze him, so he would not be able to pull the trigger. I had given him fair warning and I was about to shoot. But before I could do it, Humberto was bellowing like a bull and charging. He collided with Ahmed, knocking the rifle up and away from Sylvie, screaming, "*Diavolo! Diavolo incarnato!*"

Ahmed staggered back and collided with me. I fell against the door and smacked my head. Humberto and Ahmed were prancing back and forth, struggling in a crazy kind of dance in the middle of the floor. Sylvie had gone into the fetal position with her fists over her ears and she was still screaming a high-pitched shriek.

Then Paul was on his feet, grabbing at Humberto, trying to pull him away, shouting at him in Portuguese. I wondered, for a fraction of a second, at some people's enduring, incurable stupidity. I lunged forward, intending to ram my pistol into Ahmed's kidneys and drop him. At the same moment, Humberto wrenched the barrel of the rifle from Ahmed's left hand. Two shots in rapid succession hit the ceiling, showering the room with plaster. Ahmed staggered away from me. Humberto grabbed the rifle in both hands. Ahmed's left hand flashed. I shouted, "*Paul! No!*" But it was too late. Ahmed had plunged his hunting knife into Paul's gut. Paul staggered back, a look of shock on his face, and fell to the floor with the knife still stuck in the side of his belly.

I couldn't shoot. I had no clear line of fire, and the risk of hitting Sylvie or Mary, or Humberto, was too high. I thrust the automatic into my waistband, grabbed Ahmed by the scruff of his neck with my left hand, and pounded two powerful punches into his kidneys. He staggered, but as he did so, Humberto saw his father lying, bleeding out on the floor, and hurled himself at him, wailing in pain. I lunged again at Ahmed, but he swung the butt of the rifle and caught me a glancing blow across my temple that sent me staggering back into Dehan.

She shouted, "*Freeze!*"

The whole thing had happened in maybe four or five seconds.

Ahmed and Dehan stared at each other. In retrospect, in that moment, she should have shot him. But I guess that's what separates good people from people like Ahmed. Instead of shooting him, she waited to see if he would drop his weapon. And he, instead of dropping his weapon, aimed it at me.

I said, "Shoot the bastard. I'll take my chances."

Maybe she was about to, but that was when we heard the sirens outside. They had taken their sweet time, but the 7th Cavalry had arrived. Humberto was still wailing and shaking his motionless father. I knew when the cops got to the door, they'd hear it.

"Give it up, Ahmed. The show is over. You're surrounded, back and front. You got two ways out of here, in cuffs or in a body bag. You choose."

He started screaming again. "You shut up! You shut up! You talk I kill you! Be silent!"

Dehan spoke quietly. "You kill him, I drop you where you stand."

I glanced at the French windows. "Have a look, Ahmed."

He backed up a couple of paces so he could see. The red-and-blue lights of the patrol cars were pulsing over the garden hedge.

"Tell them to go! You tell them to go or I kill somebody."

Dehan snorted. "You move that rifle away from my partner

and I'll blow your miserable head off your damned shoulders, you piece of shit."

He was panicking, and that was all to the good. He screamed at Dehan. "Drop your weapon or I kill him!"

She smiled like she meant it. "Go ahead, make my day."

Sylvie had gone quiet. Now she sat up and got to her feet. Ahmed started screaming at her.

"What you are doing? Get down! Get down on your knees, whore!"

He was moving around like crazy while he spoke, trying to keep us both covered and stay out of Dehan's line of fire. Outside, I heard a bullhorn.

"Ahmed Abadi! We know you are in there! Put down your weapons and come outside with your hands in the air!"

The words had a strange echo and seemed to come from the back of the building as well as the front. Sylvie got on her knees beside Paul, where Humberto was sobbing with his head on his father's chest. She stroked Paul's face. Her cheeks were wet and her eyes swollen from crying. She looked up at me.

"You were right, Detective Stone. You were right. This is all my fault. It is all because of my stupidity." Then she turned to Ahmed. "Take me as your hostage."

Mary cried out, "Mom! No!"

I shook my head. "Sylvie, don't do this."

She bent and embraced Paul, enveloping him in her large, shapeless woolen cardigan. She kissed him on the lips and stood. "Take me," she said to Ahmed. "They won't let any harm come to me."

And she moved and stood in front of him.

TWENTY-FIVE

AHMED CLAMPED HIS LEFT FOREARM AROUND HER throat and placed the gun to her head. She closed her eyes and shuddered. I pulled my automatic from my waistband and aimed at his head. He swallowed. He was shaking badly.

"Now, I want a car. Tell them I want a car."

As he said it, the message was repeated on the bullhorn outside.

"*Ahmed Abadi! We know you are in there! Put down your weapons and come outside with your hands in the air!*"

"Tell them I want a car!"

Dehan curled her lip. "Screw you."

"I will kill her!"

I said, "And then what? Touch one hair on her head and we will pepper you so full of holes they'll be able to sieve spaghetti with you."

His face flushed and he shrieked, "I will hurt her! I will shoot off her toes! Her foot! I will shoot off her fingers! You think I won't? You want me to prove?"

I raised my voice. "Take it easy, jackass! I believe you. I'm reaching for my phone, okay?"

I put my automatic away and pulled my phone from my

pocket. I showed it to him and dialed the captain's number. It rang once and he answered.

"Stone! What the hell . . ."

"Listen to me, Captain. We are short of time. We have a hostage situation here."

"What?!"

"Ahmed Abadi is demanding a car to take him and his hostage, Sylvie Martin, away from here. Are you authorized to negotiate with him?"

I watched Sylvie's face while he answered, wondering what was going on inside her head. Her eyes were closed, her arms tucked inside her sleeves like a Chinese mandarin, and she looked like she was praying. The captain was saying, "Of course I am authorized! What kind of damned fool question is that? Hand me over to him and let me talk to him."

"That's what I thought. I'll explain the situation to him and get back to you."

I hung up. I had switched off the ringtone earlier. That suited me fine.

"He has to call in an NYPD negotiator. If they deem you a terrorist, it may have to go to the FBI. Either way, he is not authorized to negotiate with you."

His knees were trembling and he had big beads of sweat on his forehead. He pointed the gun down at Sylvie's right foot, but his hand was shaking so much, if he'd pulled the trigger, he'd probably have blown his own foot off.

"Call him back. Tell him. If I don't have a car in ten minutes, I start to amputate bits of this whore! Do it!"

I grabbed my phone again. The captain was trying to call me. I looked at the screen like I was about to dial, then stopped and stared into Ahmed's face.

"And then what? So you get your car. Where are you going to go? You got two choices. Canada or Mexico. Mexico, pal, they are not going to let you in. That simple. They do not give a shit. You drive over the line and they will riddle you, Sylvie, and your car so full of lead, there won't be any flesh and bones left." He swallowed. I gave him a moment to think, then went on. "So, what? Canada? You know what is going to happen there? You will have an escort of Feds all the way there—choppers, cars, and SUVs all the way. Because you will be officially ISIS. You understand that, right? And they will apply anti-terrorist rules to you. And when you get to the border, you will be surrounded on every side. You will have nowhere to go, Ahmed."

"Just do it! I swear . . ."

I laughed an ugly laugh. "And how are you going to pay for gas anyway? What are you going to eat, even if you do get out of the country?"

"Stupid American dog. I want a car, and I want one hundred thousand dollars . . ." He shook his head. "No, two hundred—two hundred and fifty thousand dollars! You make all police go back. If I see one police, I shoot off one finger. I see two police, I shoot two finger. This is Allah's justice! Eye for an eye. Make it happen!"

I called the captain.

"Stone! Did you hang up on me?"

"I explained to Ahmed that you are not authorized to negotiate, sir. But he says that unless his demands are met, he will not kill the hostage, but shoot off her toes one by one, and then her fingers. However, I am persuaded that he is willing to use deadly force as a final resort."

"Jesus! You had better let me talk to him, Stone!"

"That is what I explained to him, but he is not willing to accept it. He says his demands must be met in ten minutes or he will start amputating parts of her body."

"Stone! What is wrong with you? Let me talk to him right now!"

"Yes, sir, he wants a car with a full gas tank and two hundred and fifty thousand dollars in cash."

"Stone! This is a direct order. Let me speak to this man!"

"Yes, sir, I'll tell him."

I hung up.

"He's talking to his superiors right now. You have to understand, Ahmed, the captain has not got access to that kind of money. Even if he wanted to agree to your terms, he couldn't any more than I could. It has to go through his superiors. And there you are going to run into a problem, because within the next five minutes, you are going to be declared an ISIS terrorist, and the U.S. government does not negotiate with terrorists. See, if it had been just a car, maybe you could have gotten away with it. But now that you want the money as well, that's never going to happen."

His gun hand was trembling wildly now. His eyes were staring like crazy. "You trick me. You told me ask for money! Now you tell me money is the problem! You lie to me!"

"I'll tell you what might work, though, Ahmed."

His voice was shrill. "More tricks?"

I shook my head. "Take me as your hostage. I have more value than Sylvie because I am a senior police officer. Take me instead of her and they might just agree to your demands."

He stared at Dehan, then at me. Then he waved the gun at us each in turn. It was flapping around like a loose sail in a high wind. I had seen what Sylvie had done. I knew there was nothing I could do to stop her, so I wanted to give her the best chance of surviving that I could. Our eyes made contact for a split second and we understood each other. It was now.

I spoke in a completely flat voice as I held out my cell phone to him. "Here, you talk to him."

He cried out, "No!"

I dropped the phone, grabbed the barrel of the rifle, and levered it up. It spat three rounds into the ceiling, and as it did so, Sylvie pulled the knife from the sleeve of her cardigan and rammed it into Ahmed's thigh. Her expression was diabolical. He screamed a high-pitched screech and his leg went into spasm. She wrenched out the blade and slashed at him again. I grabbed the rifle with both hands, planted my foot on his belly, and shoved hard. He went staggering back and fell against the sofa.

Suddenly, Mary was squealing again, and Humberto had started howling like a wounded wolf. Ahmed was staggering backward, with his leg pumping blood, and jumping like a hooked fish, and Sylvie was storming after him, stabbing and slashing with the knife. I shouted at her to stop, and meanwhile Dehan went after him shouting, "*Ahmed! Freeze!*"

Instead, like the jackass he was, he turned and ran, staggering and stumbling. Sylvie went after him and so did Dehan, shouting, "Hold your fire! Hold your fire!" to the cops outside.

I was on the phone.

"Stone! What the . . . !"

"Shut up, Captain! Ahmed proceeding through back garden into church grounds. Unarmed and wounded. Pursued by Sylvie Martin! Armed and hysterical. Paul is down. Urgent medical assist! We are in pursuit! Storm the house! Repeat, storm the house!"

I hung up and ran.

As I leapt into the garden, ahead of me I could see, silhouetted against the flashing strobes of the patrol cars, the grotesque, limping figure of Ahmed, racing toward the hedge. I could hear radios crackling and voices shouting as the officers ran across the church grounds to intercept him. I could see Dehan reaching out for Sylvie, shouting at her to stop. I saw Sylvie swipe at her and push her away.

Dehan fell and I skidded to a halt beside her. "Are you okay?!"

"Yes, goddamn it! Get her!"

I ran after Sylvie. With his badly gashed leg pumping blood, Ahmed was getting weaker and slower with every step. Ahead, I saw officers, three or four of them, forcing their way through the hedge. I was closing in on Sylvie fast, but she was closing on Ahmed faster. The officers were maybe thirty feet away. Ahmed fell and Sylvie fell on top of him. I hollered, "Sylvie, don't!"

But it was too late. She was sitting astride him, holding the knife with both hands, and she plunged it into his chest, once, twice, three times. By the fourth time, I had got to her and grabbed her wrists. She was thrashing and kicking, screaming through clenched teeth as I dragged her away. The knife fell to the grass. I saw his legs twitch and blood burble from his mouth.

One of the officers knelt and felt for a pulse. He looked at me and shook his head.

"He's gone."

With a suddenness that was shocking, Sylvie screamed one last time. It was a horrible, high, shrill, histrionic sound as she glared at his dead, twitching corpse.

"You bastard! You filthy fucking bastard! May you rot in fucking hell for eternity, you fucking piece of miserable fucking shit!"

We all stared at her for a moment. Then she collapsed against me, sobbing with deep, guttural grief. I led her back to the house as the captain and his 7th Cavalry spilled out of the French windows. He hurried toward me with a scandalized look on his face. As he approached, he drew breath. I fixed him with my eyes and shook my head. He clamped his mouth shut and watched me walk past, with Sylvie in my arms and Dehan at my shoulder.

TWENTY-SIX

MAYBE PAUL'S GOD HAD BEEN LOOKING OUT FOR HIM, after all. The knife had pierced his left side and missed all his major organs. It had made a nasty cut in his abdominal muscles, but it was not life-threatening. The paramedics had insisted he should go to the hospital. He'd said he would, but after he had talked to me and given me his statement.

Ahmed was not so lucky. Sylvie had stabbed him through the sternum three times and shredded his heart like confetti. He had died instantly. There was no need for a CSI team, as we had witnessed everything in person, and after an hour, the ambulances and the squad cars left, taking with them Ahmed and the two officers he had killed when he'd slipped into the house, on his second mission to kill Sylvie.

Paul was on the sofa. Humberto was sitting next to him, holding his arm and rocking gently back and forth, muttering, "*Pater meu . . . pater meu . . .*"

My father.

Sylvie was sitting next to Humberto, and Mary was perched on the arm of the settee beside her, stroking her hair.

Dehan was sitting in the other with a "what the hell do we do now" look on her face. The captain dropped into one of the armchairs and stared at me.

"You want to explain to me, John, what just happened here?"

I nodded and looked at Sylvie for a while, wondering if she would say anything. She didn't. So I started talking.

"I have to go back to the beginning. Nineteen years ago, Simon and Sylvie Martin had a little girl in Texas. They were devout Methodists. Especially Simon. Isn't that right, Sylvie?"

She nodded, and there was an edge of irony in her voice. "He sure was devout."

"Simon worked for a large bank, the Federal United. They offered him a transfer to New York, which I am certain would have afforded him a good apartment, or a house, in just about any pleasant suburb in commuting distance of Manhattan. But Simon felt it was his duty, as a good Christian, to move to a less advantaged neighborhood, so that he and his wife could help the needy through the local church. In one of life's little ironies, it was that decision that cost him his life."

Sylvie's eyes glittered with hard, cold anger.

"That was not the only price we paid. His damned arrogance and pride cost us all our lives, one way or another."

The captain looked at her and frowned. He looked as though he was going to ask a question, but I ignored him and kept talking.

"Simon did his research and discovered that the Methodist church of St. George's was in East Brooklyn, and as luck would have it, the house that backed onto that church was for sale. With the help of his bank, he bought the house and took out very generous insurance to cover the mortgage and a good income for life for his wife, should he die for any reason. What he didn't realize was just what kind of a man the reverend was at St. George's, or just how sick his own wife had grown of his pompous, Old Testament view of marriage, life, and everything."

Paul snorted. "Where the human soul is denied its freedom, there shall hell have its dominion."

Dehan raised an eyebrow. "Who said that?"

Paul smirked. "I did."

"I am told, Captain, that Reverend Paul Truelove is, and I quote, irresistible to women. It was not long before he and Sylvie were having an affair."

I paused to draw breath, but Dehan started talking.

"It was that, plus their unwillingness to tell the truth, that made us suspect them in the beginning. It was the oldest story on Earth. Sylvie had been informed in February of the insurance coverage her husband had taken out in her favor. She knew that he was worth more to her dead than alive. She and the reverend were clearly into each other, and they were both clearly hiding something." She looked at Sylvie and shook her head. "Your amnesia story was just not credible."

"And there were other things, small details," I added. "The fact that you were holding the phone, sitting on the stairs. However you looked at it, that didn't make sense, the fact that there had been no forced entry. The weapon used was something you, Reverend, might have owned during your time in Brazil. It all pointed to you, Sylvie, having killed your own husband. Or, alternatively, the reverend killing him and you covering for him.

"That view was compounded when we discovered, Reverend, that you had lied about your whereabouts on the night of Simon's death. You told us you had been at Eastchester Bay, but in fact you had been just across the garden, and had ample opportunity to slip in, kill Simon, and get back to the church. You had motive and opportunity."

Dehan broke in again. "But somehow it didn't make a lot of sense. If you had conspired to kill him so that you could both be together, why, after eighteen years, had you not gotten married? Also, we learned from Elizabeth Cavendish that on the night of Simon's death, you had been with her, which did not suggest the actions of a man who was so in love he was ready to kill. And once you were taken out of the equation, it seemed improbable that Sylvie could have plunged that knife through Simon's sternum.

That would take a strong man. The theory that you and Sylvie had conspired with one another began to look shaky."

I nodded. "But the more we looked into it, the more it seemed possible that Humberto might have been involved. His colossal strength and his passionate, quasi-religious devotion to Sylvie made him a potentially lethal foe for anyone who might simply *seem* to be harming her. We saw it in the church, and we saw it here, tonight. We began to wonder how bad things had become between Simon and Sylvie. We discovered that Humberto used to spy on her, or at least keep watch over her. You do not realize this, Sylvie, but just a few days before Simon's death, you had a burglar in your garden. El Chato, who was on a housebreaking spree in the area, was casing your home." I turned and nodded at Humberto. "Humberto found him in the garden and chased him off.

"We wondered if El Chato had not in fact got in, Simon had interrupted him, and you had witnessed El Chato murder your husband. On the one hand, it made sense, because Humberto kept talking about how he had seen the devil in your garden and your house." I paused and looked at Sylvie for a long moment. "But then I asked myself, why would you conceal El Chato's identity? Because that was just what you were doing, wasn't it?

"For some reason, you were keeping your husband's killer's identity a secret, by pretending to have amnesia. Which kept dragging us back to the reverend. He seemed to be the only person whose identity you might want to protect. But we knew that was wrong too. Was it then that Humberto had seen you arguing with Simon and come to your rescue? Had he killed Simon defending you, and you, relieved to be free of your husband, agreed with the reverend to keep his identity secret, to protect him? There had, after all, been no evil intent. He had simply been protecting you."

Dehan sighed. "But that raised a question. It made sense in terms of the opportunity and the motivation. But where the hell would Humberto get a bowie knife? The search eventually revealed that he did in fact possess a bowie knife. It had no prints on it. But the plastic bag that contained it did have prints on it, Humberto's and somebody else's, somebody who was not in the system, not the reverend and not Sylvie or Mary. Humberto himself said that he had been given the knife by a guardian angel. Clearly, the killer had wiped his own prints off and given it to Humberto, in the bag, assuming that Humberto would take it out and handle it, thus implicating himself, and/or the reverend."

I shook my head. "But who, and why? We were out of suspects. And then it came back to me that there was somebody we had been overlooking. The gardener, Ahmed. What motive could Ahmed possibly have for wanting to kill Simon? I went and spoke to him, and he seemed a real, genuine nice guy. So much so that I almost discounted him, but, following Holmes' famous dictum, when you eliminate the impossible, whatever is left must be the truth; he was the only suspect left. He had been there that Sunday, and many other afternoons, and there was one, very feasible motive. This whole case revolved around religious fundamentalism, and religious hypocrisy.

"Ahmed had had ample opportunity to witness the reverend paying his regular visits to Sylvie. This, to Ahmed, was disgraceful behavior for a woman, and even more disgraceful for a priest. Bad enough that you were infidels, devout Christians, but that you were also engaging in fornication—that was beyond contempt. And in an act of classic religious hypocrisy, he decided he would have a bit of the action."

Sylvie was looking down at her hands clenched between her knees.

"That was why the lights were not on, wasn't it, Sylvie? That was why Simon's dinner was not ready. That was why he came through the door calling you, and you were not there to receive him. Because you were upstairs, being raped at knifepoint by Ahmed."

TWENTY-SEVEN

HER PRETTY FACE WAS TRANSFORMED INTO AN UGLY mask of grief and hatred. Her mouth pulled down at the corners, and her eyes screwed up, swollen and red, and spilled tears down her cheeks. Her voice was twisted with pain.

"Why couldn't you have just stayed out of it? Why did you have to come probing, pushing, forcing your way in? You were not welcome here!"

Mary put her arms around her and pulled her onto her lap, stroking her hair, murmuring gently to her that it would all be all right. God, she said, would make it all right.

Dehan was frowning at me. She looked confused. I met her eye for a moment. I wasn't sure if she was confused by me, or by the fact that she hadn't seen it sooner. That was the way I felt when it dawned on me. I shrugged.

"It was one of those things that is so obvious you don't see it. You represented everything that he most hated. Maybe someday, somebody will manage to explain why so many people use sex as an instrument of punishment and hate. Whatever the reason, that was what Ahmed did. He raped you. And Simon was unlucky enough to arrive home just as Ahmed was coming down the stairs.

Ahmed beat him and stabbed him to death, and left the way he'd come in, through the open back door.

"And just as his demented interpretation of 'God' had taught him that it was right to rape and subjugate you, and kill Simon, your demented interpretation taught you that it was shameful to be raped. His intention was to humiliate you, and you conspired with him by accepting that humiliation in silence."

Mary looked at me like I was being somehow grotesque.

The captain scowled. "Look here, John, that is not . . ."

I looked him in the eye. "Bullshit." I said it without any particular inflection. It was a simple statement of fact. "My job is to find and state the truth. It was the thing that kept coming up, over and over: What was it that made Sylvie conceal the identity of Simon's killer? I knew that the amnesia was a lie. I knew that she had seen his killer and she remembered who it was. What I could not understand was what was driving her to conceal it. It was not a love affair with Paul, and it was not compassion for Humberto. So what was it?

"Then it dawned on me. She was not concealing his identity. She was concealing her own shame and humiliation. She had been raped and defiled and, worse still, she had been raped and defiled by an Arab, by a Muslim. You were brought together by your own irrational hatred and contempt for each other, in an act that was supposed to be an act of love. He dressed it up as justified by his God, you concealed it under layers of hypocrisy, but you were both playing the same game. The game of divine superiority."

Mary was glaring at me. "I think she has had enough, Detective Stone!"

I shook my head. "Not quite." I paused and shook my head a second time. I felt sick, deep down sick. "Not quite. That was only the beginning of the story."

The captain looked from me to Dehan. "What? Only the beginning?"

I nodded. "It has long been a mystery to me why celibacy is supposed to be a good thing and sex is synonymous with evil." I shrugged and spread my hands. I looked at Paul. "I'd ask you to explain it—why an act that brings so much pleasure and actually creates life should be equated with evil—but I fear you might try to explain. The thing is, Simon was a staunch believer that pleasure is a bad thing and suffering and self-denial are proper emotions. They had brought one child into the world, called her Mary, and as far as he was concerned, he had done his job in that department. Am I right, Sylvie?"

She nodded. "Once, on our wedding night, and the recriminations never stopped." She spat the words out, "I committed the ultimate sin of enjoying our lovemaking! He never looked at me again! I was a harlot!"

"But you loved your daughter. Aside from the natural love you felt, I am guessing she was the only source of affection in your life, a life that had, literally, become barren. It's only a hunch, but I am pretty sure I am not wrong when I say that you longed for another child."

She nodded. "You're not wrong, Detective."

"And into that barren life—ironically, as a direct result of Simon's religious fervor—walked Reverend Paul Truelove. I don't know if you realize it, Paul, but Sylvie was trying very hard to get pregnant with your child. I don't know how you planned to explain your pregnancy to your husband, Sylvie. Maybe you planned to tell him it was an immaculate conception. He'd probably have believed you. Maybe you'd reached the point where you just didn't give a damn. I'd like to think so."

I paused. The silence in the room was a palpable presence.

"What you didn't want, what you prayed would not happen, was to get pregnant from your rapist, Ahmed."

I heard the hiss from Dehan. "*Shit!*"

Sylvie's lip trembled and she gripped onto her daughter. Mary clung to her in turn and they both started sobbing.

"You made yourself believe that Jacob was Paul's, but as the years went by, you could see it in his face. And who knows whether it was genetics or a self-fulfilling prophecy, but eventually you began to see it in his character too. And so did Ahmed. He told me himself, he ran into you in the street. I'm guessing he went out of his way, literally, to meet you in the street, and he began, over time, to recognize his own son. And maybe on some level, his son recognized him. The fact is they connected." I shrugged. "Ahmed could be a very charming, likeable guy, as I discovered myself the first time I met him. He could turn on the charm, and I bet Jacob grew to like him very quickly. They gelled. And slowly, you watched as he reeled him in. Did you try to dissuade him? I can imagine that every word you said to him against hanging out with Ahmed was another incentive to see him more often. And the deeper Ahmed and the Mullah drew him into their mosque and Islam, the more he began to see you and your church as weak and hateful. I am willing to bet that they poisoned not just his mind, but his soul."

I stopped and watched her, watched them both. They were clinging to each other, sobbing, rocking gently back and forth. I could only imagine—no, I could not begin to imagine—the pain they were both feeling. But in particular the pain that Sylvie was feeling.

The captain was staring at me, agog. But Dehan was staring at Sylvie with an expression of the deepest compassion. She spoke softly.

"So it was true. You began to draw Jacob back. What happened? Was it an intervention?" She turned to Paul, who had one hand over his eyes and was sobbing silently. "Your family, your church, united and persuaded him to come back. Of course, the penalty for that in Sharia law is death. He murdered his own son . . ."

I shook my head. "No. That wasn't what happened. Jacob converted to Islam, but he never converted back. I am guessing here, Sylvie, but I am pretty certain I am right. Ahmed had filled Jacob's heart with hatred, but you didn't want to see it. Maybe you just couldn't see it. Who can see something that ugly in their own children? How long did it go on for? A year? Two . . . ?"

Mary looked up at me, wiping her eyes with the back of her hand. "Four years."

"And you, like your mother, were too ashamed to speak out. What is this sickness in the human mind that makes us take on the shame of our attackers?" I looked down at Sylvie and felt incapable of judging her. I only hoped her jury would feel the same. "It was the day of the fête. Mary was sick in bed, and Jacob refused to go. You were in a rush, having to do everything by yourself, without help. You finally got over to your stall and realized that you had forgotten the brownies. Those damned brownies, but you were too busy to come back for them.

"It was eleven before you managed to get somebody to stand in for you. Then you hurried back. It must have been like a nightmare, coming into the house and hearing the noises from upstairs. Noises that were all too familiar. Maybe you took the knife then. Maybe Jacob had taken it up with him. I don't know, but I can imagine what happened next.

"You went up and found him raping Mary. The first clue I got was a simple slip of the tongue. You remember, Mary? You said that your mother 'came back for the brownies at eleven.' You didn't say she went back, but she came back. That placed you at home, which made sense with your bad cold, and her being so mothering and careful. I don't know whether you screamed at him or whether there was some kind of physical fight. I do know that he walked away from you. I can imagine his attitude. I have seen it in his father. Contempt and insults, calling you both whores, and I know that you rushed at him and he fell down the stairs. Maybe you pushed him in self-defense. I hope so."

The captain glanced his reproof at me. I had just handed her a defense. I didn't give a damn. I went on.

"He was dead by the time he reached the bottom of the stairs. You grabbed the knife, and I am willing to bet that you were out of your mind as you stabbed him. You were not stabbing Jacob, you were stabbing Ahmed." I turned to the captain. "Sir, my own recommendation to the DA will be not to prosecute. That will be controversial, and frankly, I don't care. I believe Jacob's killing was an act of self-defense, and I believe that Ahmed's killing tonight was partly self-defense, and partly momentary insanity brought on by unendurable provocation."

He stared at me like he didn't know whether to sack me on the spot or crucify me first. After a moment, he heaved a huge sigh. "Well, let's see what the DA says. It is certainly far from clear-cut."

I turned back to Sylvie and Mary. They had let go of each other and were frowning at me, like they didn't really understand what I had just said. I gave a smile that had more of reluctance and sadness in it than humor.

"Be smart, Sylvie, and this will soon all be over. Face it this time, see it through, and you might just be able to leave it all behind you. You have nothing to be ashamed of."

EPILOGUE

LATER THAT NIGHT, AS WE PULLED AWAY AND HEADED north once again toward Morris Park, Dehan asked me, "One thing I don't really get is why, after all these years, Ahmed suddenly decided to go after Sylvie?"

"That, I am afraid, was my bad. When I let him know today that we were onto him, he decided, rather stupidly, to eliminate the only witness to Simon's murder. He was such a stupid, arrogant ass that until then, he had enjoyed the power game of occasionally bumping into Sylvie in the street, taunting her, talking to their son, watching him grow, and knowing that he had an ever more powerful emotional grip on her. But once that grip was broken, and we were closing in on him, he decided she had to die."

We drove in silence for a few moments through the dark, empty streets. I turned right onto Morris Park without thinking.

"The lab results on the spit showed that Jacob was, indeed, Ahmed's son. And the prints I collected from him on that blank envelope . . ."

She narrowed her eyes and nodded. "I wondered why you did that."

"Yeah. They were the same as the prints on the plastic bag. Of course, Humberto knew Ahmed. He was their gardener. He was happy to accept that gift from him, considered him a guardian angel."

She nodded. "That makes sense. What about the kitchen knife? How did he get that?"

I smiled. "That was more complicated. I am guessing that Jacob took it from the block in the kitchen to threaten Mary with it. Maybe he dropped it when his mother turned up. Maybe he dropped it when he fell down the stairs. We'll never know. The thing is, she grabbed it in a rage frenzy and stabbed him. Then, I figure she wiped her prints off it and hid it. Maybe she buried it in the garden or hid it in the hedgerow and Humberto found it.

"After that, either with Paul's collusion or not—again, we'll never know—she swapped her block of knives with the block in the rectory. I checked earlier this evening. The big knife is missing, but the one we have in evidence is a perfect match."

"Son of a gun."

"Yup."

We were silent again, cruising up Morris Park toward Haight Avenue.

"There is one other thing I don't understand, Stone."

"What's that?"

"Why we are heading east on Morris Park. You live up here, but I live down on Simpson Street. Remember?"

I shook my head. "I figure I have done such a damn fine job, I deserve for you to take me out on a date. We are going to have a shower and a martini . . ." I looked at her with no particular expression and watched her eyebrows crawl up her forehead. "Separate and discreet showers and martinis, Dehan, behave yourself. And then you are going to take me to Artie's Steak and Seafood Restaurant, fifteen minutes' drive from my house."

"Oh, am I?"

"Indeed, you are. After that, we will get a taxi to my place and you will teach me your mother's recipe for margaritas."

"Ha! *That* is a family secret."

"Yeah, but I am family. We are going to get married and have twelve kids. I converted for you, remember?"

"Just twelve now? It was going to be fifteen."

"Teach me your mother's recipe for margaritas and we'll make it fifteen."

"Hmmm, it's a tempting offer, all right . . ."

**Don't miss STRANGE AND SINISTER PATH. The riveting
sequel in the Dead Cold Mystery series.**

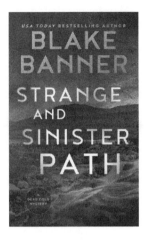

Scan the QR code below to purchase STRANGE AND SINISTER
PATH.

Or go to: righthouse.com/strange-and-sinister-path

NOTE: flip to the very end to read an exclusive sneak peak...

DON'T MISS ANYTHING!

If you want to stay up to date on all new releases in this series, with this author, or with any of our new deals, you can do so by joining our newsletters below.

In addition, you will immediately gain access to our entire *Right House VIP Library,* which includes many riveting Mystery and Thriller novels for your enjoyment!

righthouse.com/email

(Easy to unsubscribe. No spam. Ever.)

ALSO BY BLAKE BANNER

Up to date books can be found at:
www.righthouse.com/blake-banner

ROGUE THRILLERS
Gates of Hell (Book 1)
Hell's Fury (Book 2)

ALEX MASON THRILLERS
Odin (Book 1)
Ice Cold Spy (Book 2)
Mason's Law (Book 3)
Assets and Liabilities (Book 4)
Russian Roulette (Book 5)
Executive Order (Book 6)
Dead Man Talking (Book 7)
All The King's Men (Book 8)
Flashpoint (Book 9)
Brotherhood of the Goat (Book 10)
Dead Hot (Book 11)
Blood on Megiddo (Book 12)
Son of Hell (Book 13)

HARRY BAUER THRILLER SERIES
Dead of Night (Book 1)
Dying Breath (Book 2)
The Einstaat Brief (Book 3)
Quantum Kill (Book 4)
Immortal Hate (Book 5)
The Silent Blade (Book 6)
LA: Wild Justice (Book 7)

Breath of Hell (Book 8)
Invisible Evil (Book 9)
The Shadow of Ukupacha (Book 10)
Sweet Razor Cut (Book 11)
Blood of the Innocent (Book 12)
Blood on Balthazar (Book 13)
Simple Kill (Book 14)
Riding The Devil (Book 15)
The Unavenged (Book 16)
The Devil's Vengeance (Book 17)
Bloody Retribution (Book 18)
Rogue Kill (Book 19)
Blood for Blood (Book 20)

DEAD COLD MYSTERY SERIES
An Ace and a Pair (Book 1)
Two Bare Arms (Book 2)
Garden of the Damned (Book 3)
Let Us Prey (Book 4)
The Sins of the Father (Book 5)
Strange and Sinister Path (Book 6)
The Heart to Kill (Book 7)
Unnatural Murder (Book 8)
Fire from Heaven (Book 9)
To Kill Upon A Kiss (Book 10)
Murder Most Scottish (Book 11)
The Butcher of Whitechapel (Book 12)
Little Dead Riding Hood (Book 13)
Trick or Treat (Book 14)
Blood Into Wine (Book 15)
Jack In The Box (Book 16)
The Fall Moon (Book 17)
Blood In Babylon (Book 18)
Death In Dexter (Book 19)
Mustang Sally (Book 20)

A Christmas Killing (Book 21)
Mommy's Little Killer (Book 22)
Bleed Out (Book 23)
Dead and Buried (Book 24)
In Hot Blood (Book 25)
Fallen Angels (Book 26)
Knife Edge (Book 27)
Along Came A Spider (Book 28)
Cold Blood (Book 29)
Curtain Call (Book 30)

THE OMEGA SERIES
Dawn of the Hunter (Book 1)
Double Edged Blade (Book 2)
The Storm (Book 3)
The Hand of War (Book 4)
A Harvest of Blood (Book 5)
To Rule in Hell (Book 6)
Kill: One (Book 7)
Powder Burn (Book 8)
Kill: Two (Book 9)
Unleashed (Book 10)
The Omicron Kill (Book 11)
9mm Justice (Book 12)
Kill: Four (Book 13)
Death In Freedom (Book 14)
Endgame (Book 15)

ABOUT US

Right House is an independent publisher created by authors for readers. We specialize in Action, Thriller, Mystery, and Crime novels.

If you enjoyed this novel, then there is a good chance you will like what else we have to offer! Please stay up to date by using any of the links below.

Join our mailing lists to stay up to date --> righthouse.com/email
Visit our website --> righthouse.com
Contact us --> contact@righthouse.com

facebook.com/righthousebooks
x.com/righthousebooks
instagram.com/righthousebooks

EXCLUSIVE SNEAK PEAK OF...

STRANGE AND SINISTER PATH

CHAPTER 1

THE CAPTAIN WANDERED INTO THE DETECTIVES' ROOM looking like a surprised ostrich lost in Times Square at rush hour. He rarely descended from the remote heights of his office upstairs. Now he inched through the room, looking right and left until he saw me watching him. He waved and moved my way. When he was within earshot I said to Dehan, who was reading through cold case files, "Don't say anything rude about the captain."

She frowned at the page in front of her like she wasn't really listening. "Why?"

"Because he's right behind you."

She jumped and looked around. I smiled. "Guilty conscience, Dehan."

The captain still wore his air of ratite uncertainty. "Good morning, you two. How's tricks?"

I offered him no expression and said, "She hasn't come in this morning, sir."

His eyebrows twitched, and he placed a file on the desk. After a moment, he sat and nodded, like he'd got the joke but didn't think it was especially funny. "We have an unusual request from the sheriff of Lee County, in Colorado."

I couldn't think of anything to say, but Dehan dropped the

case she was reading and frowned. "Lee County? Colorado? Really? What's the request?"

"The details are in the file"—he patted the file with his palm —"but in a nutshell, Detectives, Kathleen Olvera, of Rosedale Avenue, just down the road here, aged twenty-three, was found in Lefthand Canyon . . ."

Dehan laughed. The captain looked at her like she'd said something inappropriate. She suppressed the laugh. "Lefthand Canyon? Seriously?"

"There was nothing funny about the way she was found, Detective Dehan. She had been clubbed, strangled, raped, and then decapitated. This was back in 2012. There was some uncertainty over jurisdiction . . ."

I leaned forward. "Why?"

"Because it wasn't clear that she had been killed there."

I scratched my head. "It's not very likely that she was killed here and transported over one and a half thousand miles to Colorado."

"Quite. I agree. And as the actual scene of the crime was never discovered, the local sheriff investigated. However, there was very little evidence, and eventually the case went cold."

"So what's his request?"

"The Denver DA wanted a review of cold cases, and as they were not able to make any progress, and Kathleen was originally from here, he has asked me if I wanted to run it by *our* cold-cases team."

I raised my eyebrows and spread my hands. "Sure. We'll take a look, see what we come up with. But if it turns out to be a Lee County, Colorado, case, we're going to end up batting it right back to the sheriff."

He nodded, then made a peculiar smile with the corners of his eyes. "Have a look. See what you come up with."

He left us and wandered around the detectives' room for a bit, peering at things and smiling with an air of it all coming back to him, then retired upstairs. You got the feeling he'd had quite enough excitement for one morning.

I picked up the file, and Dehan snatched it from my fingers. She leaned back in her chair and put her boots on the corner of the desk. Her legs were as long as an eight-day week. She read aloud while I sat back and enjoyed looking at her.

"Kathleen Olvera, twenty-three, married to Moses Olvera, then twenty-four, of Seven Hills, Colorado . . ."

"Ah!"

"Don't interrupt. Mother of newborn Sin-eed—S-I-N-E-A-D —how do you pronounce that?"

"Shin-aid."

"What is it, Irish?"

"Uh-huh."

"Kathleen, Sinead, these guys are Irish. Okay. So according to testimony given by Moses and Kathleen's mother, Melanie Vuolo, in July of 2012, Kathleen was suffering from postpartum depression and decided to take a few days and go visit Moses' parents, in Seven Hills. That was Friday the sixth. The parents-in-law, that's Alfredo and Ingrid, claim she never showed up. A few days later, some trekkers found her body abandoned in the woods and called the sheriff. He administered a rape kit because her clothes were in disarray. Her blouse had been ripped and the zipper on her skirt was broken . . ."

"What?"

She glanced at me. "The zipper on her skirt had been broken." She continued reading. "Only one of her shoes was found at the scene. The other was recovered later, on the Lee Hill Road, half a mile outside Boulder."

"Hmmm . . ."

"Shut up. The rape kit established that she had had sex before being killed. Impossible to tell whether it was consensual or not because, after a week in the open, in warm weather, the body was badly deteriorated and partly eaten by animals. The semen was too deteriorated and contaminated to provide a hit. The head was found about six feet from the body..." She pulled out an eight-by-ten photograph, examined it, and tossed it over to me. "It had been severed surgically, with a single, clean cut, no hacking or sawing. The weapon was not found. There was evidence of blunt force trauma to the back of the head, premortem." She sighed. "A few initial suspects..."

I held up a hand. "Stop there. Let's not follow the same mistaken tracks that they did. Let's pursue our own thoughts. Anything strike you? Where do you want to start?"

We stared at each other for a few long seconds. It was a habit we had got into which irritated other people, but it helped us to think. Eventually she said, "Let's talk to the mother. She lives on Commonwealth Avenue"—she checked the file—"and so do Isaac and Anne-Marie. That's Moses' brother and his wife. They seem to have been a close-knit family." She shrugged. "Catholics. Kathleen's postpartum depression seems to be what sent her off to Colorado, and eventually her death. One person she is most likely to have talked to about it is her mother. Let's start there."

"Hmmm..."

"You've never been a mother, you wouldn't know."

"Or a daughter. Let's go, Little Grasshopper. Let's go talk to Melanie Vuolo. It's not a bad place to start."

OCTOBER WAS FEELING TOO lazy after the long, warm months to move over and let in the cold. The leaves on the trees were turning copper but were in denial about their age, and the whole of New York was pretending it was still summer. So we decided to walk the half mile to Commonwealth Avenue at an easy stroll. Along the way, Dehan talked.

"So. She lives in the Bronx but she dies in the Rockies. Is that a random event, or is there a direct causal link? Her husband is from Colorado, she claims she is going to see *his* parents..." She shrugged and spread her hands while making a "what can I say?" face. "Maybe they got on well. She has her own mother here, but maybe she gets on with the in-laws. It's not common, but it happens. However that may be, the fact that she never turns up has got to raise the question, was visiting the in-laws just an excuse? Was she really going to meet somebody else?"

"That's two questions."

"Don't interrupt me, Stone. I'm having a flow. We need more facts. We need to know, what was her relationship like with the in-laws? Did she meet her husband in Colorado, or here in New York? If it was out there, who else did she meet?"

"Whom."

"What?"

"Whom else did she meet."

"Uh-huh . . . also, her depression." She shook her head.

"What about it?"

She sucked air through her teeth. "You can't generalize, I know, but the normal thing is, if a girl is depressed after childbirth, she turns to her mother. She doesn't put one and a half thousand miles between herself and her mother. Know what I mean? I mean, if she and the in-laws live *that* far apart, how close can they be, right?"

"Fair point."

"So, my gut, which you are always saying I should listen to, is saying this was not a random killing. She was in Colorado not for the in-laws, but for somebody else." She raised an eyebrow at me. "*Cherchez l'homme.*"

I smiled. "Unless she was a lesbian. In which case, *cherchez la femme.*"

"Right. Here we are. It's that one over there."

It was basically a large, redbrick box with a very small patch of garden out front, sitting behind a very large, old chestnut tree. Directly opposite there was a row of much bigger redbrick boxes, in the form of a complex of apartment blocks that were probably about a hundred years old. They were surrounded by wrought iron fences that hadn't stopped kids from spraying the old walls with ugly, uninspired graffiti. They thought of themselves as artists, but most of them seemed capable only of painting their signatures.

I had stopped to look around while Dehan climbed the steps and rang on the bell. It had once been a solid, working-class area. But decades of Don't Give a Damn had reduced it to a dystopian wilderness where adults hid indoors from a world they no longer understood, while their kids bought into the myth that, in an ugly world, the smartest thing you can do is make it uglier.

The door was opened by a dark, frowning woman in her fifties. Dehan showed her her badge as I climbed the steps.

"Mrs. Vuolo? Melanie Vuolo?"

The woman shook her head. "No, she don't live here no more. She ain't lived here for maybe four years."

Dehan smiled and put her badge away. "Really? Do you know where she's gone?"

"Yeah, she was buying a place up in Morris Park. I got the address somewhere, to forward her mail."

She stared at us a moment, while we smiled politely back. Finally I said, "Could you let us have it?"

"Yeah, is nine twenty, Van Nest. She say is a nice big house, but she never invite me to go see it. She in trouble? I know her daughter died. And the baby was just a few weeks old. That was a big tragedy for her."

I nodded. "Were you friends?"

"No."

"Do you know if her son-in-law moved too? Or are they still here?" I glanced at the block behind us.

"No. They all gone together. Whole family."

Dehan frowned. "The son-in-law moved with the mother?"

"All of them. They all gone together."

We thanked her for her help and started back up the road toward the station, under the big chestnuts and the lazy blue sky. After a while Dehan said, "Catholics and Jews."

There wasn't much I could answer to that, so I smiled benignly at the trees instead. She considered me a moment. When she saw I wasn't going to ask what she meant, she told me anyway. "The whole family thing. With Jews and Catholics, the family acquires an identity all its own, above and beyond the people who constitute it. It's like a corporation. In law, a corporation has its own, separate identity. Catholic and Jewish families are like that. Each family has its own, unique identity. When a tragedy happens, the family takes over. Something great happens, the family takes over. Birth, marriage, death . . . the family."

She paused, stuck her hands in her back pockets, and watched her feet moving beneath her. "Kathleen died. If she hadn't died, she would eventually have become the matriarch, the family figurehead, and people would have said, 'Oh, she's just like her mother!' Instead of that, she died, so her mother took over. And when she moved, I guess she took the whole family with her. Loyalty. Loyalty to the family. It's a big deal for Catholics and Jews. It can be a thing of beauty, or it can be a nightmare."

My car is a thing of beauty. It's a burgundy 1964 Jaguar Mark II, original right-hand drive, 210 bhp. I observed it fondly now as we approached and asked Dehan, "You think that might be relevant?"

She walked around to the passenger side and waited for me to unlock the door, staring up at the cloudless sky.

"It's usually relevant to everything. So yeah, maybe."

I thought maybe she was right. We climbed in and headed toward Morris Park.

CHAPTER 2

MELANIE VUOLO'S NEW HOUSE WAS A BIG, WHITE, detached clapboard affair a couple of blocks from Van Nest Park. She opened the door and didn't so much look at us as calibrate us. She had mischievous eyes and a naughty smile to go with it. She had red hair, deep blue eyes, and a cute spray of freckles across her nose. She was probably in her midfifties, but looked younger. She raised an eyebrow at Dehan and almost winked at me. Her eyelid fluttered, but she thought better of it and smiled instead. Like I said, it was a naughty smile.

"Yes?"

We showed her our badges.

"I am Detective Stone, this is Detective Dehan. May we come in, please, Mrs. Vuolo?"

The change in her expression said she guessed why we were there. She stood back, watching my face. "Is it about Kath? Have you caught the bastard?"

Her accent was Irish. Not New York Irish, but Irish Irish.

"No, not yet, but the Lee County sheriff has asked us to look into a few things at this end."

She gave a quick nod. "Come in. Would you have a cup of tea?" Before I could answer she looked up into Dehan's face.

"How 'bout you, love? Will you have a nice cup of tea? I'll put the kettle on, so. Go and sit down. I'll be with you in no time. Isn't the weather awful unseasonal?"

The living room was at the back, which made it dark. Through the French doors, the back garden was a luminous green, with the shadow of the house cast long across the grass, touching a large, old wooden shed at the end. The room was fussily furnished, with lots of lace and small porcelain statues of kittens looking nauseating. There were photographs, dozens of them, on every available surface. I scanned them and took note, but Dehan was working through them methodically, one after another. Melanie's voice came to us from the kitchen.

"Would you have some biscuits? What biscuits do you like? Sure, I'll put out a selection, shall I?"

She came in on busy feet with a laden tray and set it on the coffee table in front of the fireplace. "Don't stand there like a couple of trees," she said. "Sit. Milk and sugar? Help yourself to biscuits. The chocolate ones are my favorites."

She laughed for no particular reason as she poured from a large, elaborate teapot. Dehan sat in an armchair, and Melanie handed her an elaborate cup of the same design. Dehan took it and cleared her throat.

"Mrs. Vuolo . . ."

"Mel."

"Mel, what can you tell us about Kath? What made her go to Colorado? How were things at home with her and . . . ? No milk or sugar."

"Mo." She said it as she filled my cup. I sat and she handed it to me. "He's a lovely fellow." Her smile was genuine. "Didn't he just dote on her! *Nothing* was too much for him. God forgive me for saying it, but she didn't know what she had!"

Dehan bit into a biscuit and spoke with her mouth full. "She was depressed?"

"God love her. Ever since little Sinead was born. Between you and me, I think it was an accident. She wouldn't take the pill, you see? And I know you fellers . . ." She waved a finger at me. "You don't like the condoms." She turned back to Dehan. "They say they can't feel anything. Well, I mean, what's to feel? But all the same, that's what most fellers say, according to Mo. I wouldn't know. I always took the pill. Tony, that was my husband, God rest him, he insisted on it. He was awful demanding. An Italian." She turned back to me. "Italians are awful passionate, you know. No offense." She smiled and reached out a hand to touch my knee.

"Mel, tell us about Kath's depression."

"Well, that's what I'm saying! I don't think she was ready to have a baby. Of course, when I was young, we had no time to get depressed, but nowadays it's different, isn't it? And after little Sinead was born, didn't poor Kath get awful low."

Dehan sipped and asked, "How did that affect her relationship with Mo?"

"Well, it wasn't ideal, was it? But then, when is marriage ideal? You know, marriage was not intended to be a magic panacea for happiness, was it?" She turned to me as though I might want to answer. "It was intended to be a partnership, and like all partnerships, there will be good and bad times. But, God love 'em both, things were not easy for them."

"How's that?"

"Poor Mo was working construction. Him and Isaac both. And just after Sinead was born, didn't the fecking foreman go and fire Mo, with a newborn baby at home an' all. He looked everywhere for work, but God bless the boy, hard as he looked, he couldn't find a thing. But even with that, the two of them were inseparable. They just doted on each other. Did everything together, went everywhere together . . ."

Dehan raised an eyebrow. "Except Colorado." Mel looked surprised, but Dehan pressed on. "What's the Colorado connection, Mel? It's an awful long way to go and find a husband."

Mel smiled and sighed. "And isn't *that* the truth! It was Tony, my husband. He was Italian, like I say, and he was crazy about the westerns! Don't they call them spaghetti westerns because the Italians love'm so much? Well! He couldn't get enough of the damn things! So when the girls were small we used to go on holiday to 'cowboy country.' He worked all the hours that God sent and he made a decent living for us. But he insisted, on the holidays, we had to go west: Texas, Arizona, North and South Dakota, Wyoming . . . and in the end we went to Colorado. The girls were twelve and thirteen. And we went to Boulder and every fecking day . . . !" She hooted with laughter. "*Every fecking day* he'd drag us up into the mountains, till we found this town, Seven Hills. Well, you'd love it! Wasn't it straight out of the movies! With a saloon and everything! So we cancelled the B and B in Boulder and spent the rest of the holiday in Seven Hills, in the saloon. Booked a couple of rooms there."

"And that's where she met Mo?"

"And Isaac and Greg."

I raised my eyebrows as I reached for another biscuit. "Greg?"

"Isaac and Mo are brothers. Lovely lads, lovely parents, Ingrid and Alfredo. He was Mexican, but a lovely fellow all the same. And Greg was their friend. His father had a ranch nearby. They was forever together, playing and getting into all sorts of trouble. Happy-go-lucky as you like. Lovely lads. Well, didn't we end up going back every year after that?"

"What happened to your husband, Mel?"

"An accident at work took him from us, 2005. They tried to say that he was careless, but my Tony was never careless. He was meticulous in everything." She sipped her tea. "He left us cared for, all the same, and the company settled out of court. I mean to say, would they settle out of court if it was his fault? I don't think so, do you? Bastards."

"So you continued going to Seven Hills."

"Well, we had to, didn't we? For his memory, and also because the girls loved it there. It's a different world. The freedom! And it's clean, and the people are—no offense—well, they're kind and honest and decent. Not like, you know, a lot of people in the city. And didn't they love their little friends?"

Dehan said, "Kath would have been fifteen?"

Mel nodded. "And I think that was when she fell in love with Mo. It was Isaac at first, when they were kids, and we always said that Isaac and Kath would end up together, and Mo and Pat. And poor Greg, well, he had nobody. But that summer it all changed, and to be honest, I think Isaac was a bit upset. It was okay in the end, because he married Anne-Marie, who's a lovely girl. Just lovely!" She sighed. "But Mo had grown in just a year into a very handsome young man, and he was funny, you know? Had a great sense of humor. All the girls were crazy about him. And she being so upset about her father, he made her laugh." She turned to Dehan. "That counts for a lot, doesn't it, love? When a man can make you laugh."

Dehan's cup was empty. She put it on the table and took another biscuit. "So what happened to Pat?"

Mel's face seemed to contract in on itself. For a moment it looked as though she might start crying, but there was a strength there that held her in check. She waited a moment, then took a deep breath.

"They were both hit real hard by Tony's death. Kath was lucky in that she found love and consolation with Mo. God love him, he was a rock for her. But Pat wasn't so fortunate, and she . . ." She stopped and stared out of the French windows, at the unseasonal sunshine. "She got in with the wrong crowd. Greg was a good lad, but he had some bad friends. Pat started drinking, and then it was the pot, smoking pot, and then it was the hard stuff."

I asked, "Where is she now?"

"She's been dry for a couple of years now, staying off the pot and that. She's out with friends."

"She lives at home with you?"

She burst out laughing. It was a startling sound, almost like the screech of a parrot. "Sure! Don't they all feckin' live at home with me! *Jaysus!* What I wouldn't give for them to all feck off and get their own feckin' places! But they're all still at home with mummy!"

She fell back on the sofa laughing. It was infectious, and I glanced at Dehan. She was laughing too.

When she'd settled a bit, I asked, "Who is 'all'?"

"Ah, love'm. I know life is hard these days, and I don't begrudge them. Mo and, uh"—she hesitated—"and Sinead, they're living at home. He's working at the car dealer and she's started the nursery. Pat's at home, you know, she can't look after herself. She just slips back and starts drinking and smoking again, and mixing with the wrong crowd..."

I smiled, thinking of Dehan's prediction about the matriarch. "What about Isaac and . . ."

"Oh, well, that didn't work out. Him and Anne-Marie broke up."

"When was that?"

"Just a couple of months after Kath . . . you know, was . . ."

I nodded. "I see." I pointed at one of the photographs. Dehan was already nodding, like she had wanted to ask the same question. "I notice a picture there. I gather that's Mo, because there are several of him with Kath. But there he is not with Kath. Who is that girl?"

She looked a bit embarrassed. "Well, that's Anne-Marie." She took a deep breath. "Kath's death was a terrible upheaval for all of us. A second tragedy, and it seemed not so long ago that Tony had died." She shrugged and shook her head. The gesture seemed to say that it was just one of those things. "Mo was devastated. Anne-Marie was just *there* for him. A tower of strength. He'd lost his job, Isaac was working . . . one thing led to another . . ."

I nodded again. "It always does. So Anne-Marie is living here too?"

"Yes. She and Mo were married last year."

Dehan smiled at her. "So you are helping them to rebuild their lives."

"I'm doing what I can, love. In hard times, family has to pull together. All you've got is your family, and thank God we have each other."

I pulled my notepad from my pocket. "We are going to need to talk to Mo. Where can we find him?"

"Him and Anne-Marie are both at the Used Car Mart on 177th Street. She does the paperwork and he sells the cars."

I made a note. "How about Isaac?"

"The last I heard from Isaac, he was living out in Hunts Point. Poor love, things didn't go so well for him. He works for a building supplies company on Halleck Street. Leastwise, he did. He rents an apartment at 841 Longfellow Avenue, bless him."

I glanced at Dehan. She shook her head, so I stood.

"Thank you, Mel. You have been very helpful. We may have to talk to you again at some point, or to Pat. But we'll try not to disturb you."

She told us it was no trouble at all and showed us to the door. We stepped out into the warm fall midday and heard the door close behind us. Dehan walked around to the passenger side of the car and leaned on the roof, watching me unlock the door.

"I need a beer," she said. "And so do you."

CHAPTER 3

We drove east along Van Nest as far as Bronxdale, then turned north. We had the windows open and cruised at a nice, easy speed, enjoying the temperature. We didn't talk for a bit, till I glanced at her and asked, "Impressions?"

She had her elbow out the window. Her hair was streaming across her face, so she reached back and tied it in a knot at the back of her head. It looked good, but she was totally oblivious to the fact. She was the best-looking woman I had ever met, and also the least vain. She turned to face me and I saw myself duplicated, looking back at myself from her aviators.

"I gotta say, Stone, I didn't get a damn thing." She shrugged. "Mo? Killed her so he could be with Anne-Marie?" She made a face and shook her head. "That's stupid, especially as Anne-Marie went and divorced Isaac just a few months later. Mo could have done the same. Besides, she was killed in Colorado."

I nodded once. "I agree. But we should find out where he was at the time anyway. What about Isaac?"

She made a face like she'd just smelled sour milk. I pulled over and parked outside The Grill House. We pushed in and ordered two beers and a couple of hamburgers, then grabbed a table near the window.

Dehan took a pull and gave herself a froth moustache, which I didn't tell her about. "You know what?" she said. "If Mo had been killed, I'd be looking at Isaac. But that would have happened a long time ago. Why would he kill her after she gave birth? And why would he go all the way to Colorado to do it?"

I took a pull on my beer and sighed noisily through my nose. She pointed at me and grinned. "You have a moustache."

I wiped it away with the back of my hand and smiled back. "That reasoning applies to everybody she knew in New York. I am not convinced that her depression was exclusively postpartum. I think there may have been more going on in her life that we don't know about. There's a connection here between her depression, her trip to Seven Hills, and her death." I paused and pointed at her. "Speaking of which, I was surprised you didn't ask her more about Kath's depression."

"You didn't either."

"You first."

She squinted out the window, like the view didn't quite convince her. "I don't know, Stone. She didn't seem to me to be quite in touch with reality. In fact, I get the feeling she'll go to any lengths to *avoid* an unpleasant reality."

I laughed.

She ignored me and went on. "Kath and Mo doted on each other. They were crazy about each other. He was mad about her and he was so supportive. But when they have a baby, she goes into a depression and goes to Colorado, and when she gets murdered, he marries his brother's wife." She shrugged. "Maybe I'm being judgmental, but that doesn't sound to me like a couple who are doting on each other and are crazy about each other."

I was nodding. "So your point is?"

"I think if I had asked her about Kath's depression, I would have heard what Mel wanted to believe about her depression. And I already know that. The useful information is going to come from Mo and Pat, and maybe Anne-Marie. That what you were thinking?"

"Yup."

The burgers arrived and she took a big bite, spilling salad on her plate. She spoke around a mouthful of meat and bun.

"Sho wha-oo wa' do mow?"

I ate for a while without answering her, watching the anonymous people hurrying past on the sidewalk, wondering how a cute young mother from the Bronx winds up dead, beheaded, and probably raped in the woods in Lefthand Canyon in Colorado. What was the sequence of events that led to her death? At what point did she tip the domino that led, irrevocably, to her murder? Did it happen here, or there?

I wiped my mouth as she drained her beer. "I guess," I said, and leaned forward with a fresh paper napkin, "we go and talk to Mo." As I said it, I carefully wiped the froth from her upper lip. She watched me with a curious mixture of alarm and amusement in her huge, brown eyes. I smiled. "You had a Santa Claus moustache."

It was a short drive down White Plains to East Tremont, and then onto East 177th. It's a grim, soulless part of the Bronx, with gray concrete wastelands as far as the eye can see. And if you move off the avenue, into the back streets, you find decaying red brick and rusting iron, boarded-up windows and graffiti, and the haunted eyes of people who don't even despair, because hopelessness is the only thing they have ever known.

I pulled up on the stark, gray forecourt and we climbed out. The air smelled of exhaust fumes and thrummed with the steady flow of trucks and cars on the avenue and the four freeways that surrounded it. Nobody stopped here. People only passed through, in a hurry.

As we slammed the doors, a man in his late twenties or early thirties stepped out. He was good-looking in a Latin kind of way, with brown eyes, dark curly hair, and a shiny suit that was too baggy and probably too expensive. He smiled with very white teeth and nodded at the Jag.

"Nice wheels. You looking to sell it?"

"Not while I can still drive. I'm looking for Moses Olvera." I showed him my badge. "That you?"

For a moment, he looked worried. "Sure. Is there a problem?"

"We just wanted to ask you some questions about Kathleen."

His eyebrows shot up. "Kath? Well . . ." He looked from me to Dehan and back again. "Kath is dead. She died five years ago . . ."

Dehan frowned at him. "That's why we want to ask you about her, Mo."

He gave a small, nervous laugh. "But that was in Colorado."

I studied his face a moment, trying to read what was going on behind it. Finally, I said, "Is there somewhere we can talk?"

"Well sure, come on into the office. Anne-Marie is there . . ."

"We'd like to talk to her too."

He led us out of the glare and the noise into a cool, shaded interior where everything was shiny: the floors, the plate glass windows, the cars—his suit and his teeth fit right in there. We followed him across the showroom and into a small office at the back. Anne-Marie looked up and smiled as we came in. She was an attractive woman with blond hair and dark blue eyes. She had a natural elegance that was missing in Mo.

"Good afternoon."

I smiled back and showed her my badge. "You Anne-Marie?" The smile faded, and she turned to Mo before answering, like she was checking with him. "Yes. What is this about?"

There was a small table with four chairs around it set to one side, where customers could sit and sign their contracts of sale. Mo gestured us to it and Anne-Marie joined us. As she did so, Dehan spoke.

"The Lee County Sheriff's Department has asked us to make some inquiries on their behalf regarding Kath's murder five years ago."

Mo sat slowly, as though he was somehow deflating. He said, "Oh . . . I thought we had left that all behind us."

Anne-Marie reached out and touched his arm. She held his hand and stroked his hair. "How could it be, sugar? They never caught who did it, did they? They ain't gonna stop till they do." She turned to smile at Dehan. "Are you?"

I said, "The colder a case gets, the more difficult it becomes to solve it. But we never give up."

Dehan put her elbows on the table and sucked her teeth. "What we're really interested in at the moment is Kath's state of mind when she went to Seven Hills. What made her do that, all on her own, with a newborn baby . . . ?"

"Maybe you'd better answer that, sugar." Anne-Marie turned to Mo. "You knew better than I did."

There were some glossy brochures on the table, and now he moved them about a bit, as though he didn't like the way they fit and he was trying to organize them into a better arrangement. "This's kind of come out of left field. I'm not sure . . ."

Dehan had her eyes narrowed at him, like she was trying to peer through a dense fog. "Is that a difficult question, Mo?"

He flushed and looked straight at her. "No! No, I guess not. It's just unexpected, after all this time."

I gave him an understanding smile and said, "Sure. The report said she was depressed."

He nodded. "She was. Postpartum depression. After Sinead was born, she got real low. I didn't know what to do to help her. We were real close always, ever since her pa died. But then everything seemed to kind of change when Baby came along." He shrugged and glanced at Anne-Marie, as though seeking support and confirmation. "We hadn't really planned on having a baby yet. My work wasn't real secure. In fact, I got fired just after Baby was born. And Kath was worried about having kids if we wasn't financially secure. She was sound like that."

Dehan raised an eyebrow. "How did you feel about the baby?"

His face lit up. "Oh, I was over the moon. She was the cutest thing you can imagine. Still is."

I smiled, like I shared his pleasure. "Mo, can you think of anything besides the birth of the baby that might have been depressing Kath?"

His smile faded. "Not really. I mean, we had our money problems, and that was getting to both of us, but we was solid, and we had the family right by us, didn't we?" He turned to Anne-Marie, and she took his hand.

Dehan studied her a moment. "Did she ever confide in you, Anne-Marie? Did she ever talk to you about what was troubling her?"

Anne-Marie nodded vigorously. "Oh, Lord, yeah. We was real close. We was almost like sisters. She would tell me most everything. Even told me a few secrets about this feller!" They laughed, and we smiled patiently. "But when this depression came on her, she just clammed right up. She wouldn't talk to Mo and she wouldn't talk to me. In a sense, that was what started me and Mo getting close, 'cause we used to talk about her, and what was wrong with her. And so we kind of come together."

Dehan raised an eyebrow. "So were you two seeing each other before . . ."

They both erupted simultaneously, and the look of horror on their faces seemed genuine.

"Oh, *Lord* no!"

Then Mo added, "We became close as *friends*. But what really brought us together was when poor Kath died. Then Anne-Marie was a real consolation. She was my tower of strength. But we spoke to Isaac before we ever took it any further than holding hands. We never went behind his back, or Kath's."

I scratched my chin. "Here's the thing we can't understand. What would make Kath take off and travel one and a half thousand miles across the country, when her mother and her whole family was right here?"

He nodded a few times, like he was saying the question made

sense, but had a reasonable answer. "What she said to me and her ma was that she needed to get away from me and Baby for a few days. We didn't have money for her to go on a weekend break or anything, so she was going to go and visit my parents. She got on real well with Ingrid and Alfredo."

Dehan's eyebrows shot up. "Ingrid and Alfredo?"

"My parents."

"I know. You don't call them Mom and Dad?"

He gave a sheepish grin. "I guess we never did. Ingie was kind of strict that way. Ingie, my mom."

"So . . ." I scratched my chin again. "Kath had a good relationship with Ingrid and Alfredo."

"Yeah, they loved her, got on real well."

"When was the last time she had seen them, Mo?"

"Oh, well, that would be a couple of years. Since we moved out here."

"You and Isaac."

"And Anne-Marie."

Anne-Marie spoke before I could ask. "Me and Isaac got married just before we all three moved out together. Mel was real helpful and supportive. She helped Isaac get his construction job before we come. Then *he* helped Mo."

I nodded for a bit, drumming my fingers on the table. Dehan asked, "How did Isaac take Kath's death?"

Anne-Marie's face hardened for a moment, then she shrugged. "It hit us all real hard. He was upset, like the rest of us."

"Do you stay in touch?"

Mo shook his head. "Not really. It was hard for him."

There was something ruthless in Dehan's voice when she said, "Triple blow for him, huh? His childhood sweetheart, his wife, and his brother."

They both looked down at the table. Unconsciously, Anne-Marie reached for Mo's hand. He gave a small shrug. "I guess that's just the way the cookie crumbled. We didn't mean him no harm."

I patted the glossy brochures with my palm a couple of times. "Sure. Listen, you've been very helpful. We may need to talk to you again. I hope that's not a problem."

Mo smiled, but Anne-Marie was still staring down at the table. She hadn't liked Dehan's crack. Mo said, "Anything we can do to help, Detectives."

We left them in the office and stepped out through the shiny showroom and into the mellow afternoon, where the shadows were growing long as the sun began to sink in the southwest. We climbed into the car and eased into the flow of traffic. Dehan eyed me and said, "Isaac?"

I frowned and shook my head, then nodded. "Call him, will you?" I reached in my pocket and handed her the details Mel had given me. "Ask him to come in to the station. I have a feeling he is going to have quite a lot to tell us. This loving, close-knit family is hiding something, and Isaac might be just the man to tell us what."

Dehan was dialing. "Yup. My feelings exactly, Sensei."

Scan the QR code below to purchase STRANGE AND SINISTER PATH.
Or go to: righthouse.com/strange-and-sinister-path

Made in the USA
Las Vegas, NV
01 March 2025